THE AMISH WIDOWER'S DILEMMA

CHRISTINA RICH

PLEASE RECYCLE
THIS PRODUCT IS RECYCLABLE

Recycling programs for this product may not exist in your area.

ISBN-13: 978-1-335-52910-7

The Amish Widower's Dilemma

For questions and comments about the quality of this book, please contact us at CustomerService@Harlequin.com.

Love Inspired
22 Adelaide St. West, 41st Floor
Toronto, Ontario M5H 4E3, Canada
www.LoveInspired.com

HarperCollins Publishers
Macken House, 39/40 Mayor Street Upper,
Dublin 1, D01 C9W8, Ireland
www.HarperCollins.com

Printed in Lithuania

1 2 3 4 5 6 7 8 9 10 LIT 28 27 26 25

“Give me the summer, Noah,” Lydia pleaded.

Was she the answer to his prayers?

He shifted his weight. “Two weeks.”

Her shoulders sank. “That’s not enough time.”

“It’s what I’m willing to give you.” Any more than that and he might start longing for fellowship with the community again—with her. And he couldn’t subject Jacob to ridicule.

She released a heavy sigh. “Four.”

He started to argue, but she held up her free hand.

“But, if you see changes in Jacob, you give me more time.”

“No. This is a bad idea. We will be fine,” he said, reaching out to take Jacob’s hand. His son dug his heels into the dirt and grunted as he clawed at Lydia’s arm. “You should go.”

“No go. No go,” Jacob cried as he stomped his feet.

“Noah, please.”

Lydia’s soft whisper threatened to implode his resolve to stand firm.

“No,” he said, shaking his head. He swept his kicking son into his arms and held him tight against his side. “Goodbye, Lydia.”

Christina Rich lives in northeast Kansas. Her passion for stories comes from a rich past of reading and digging through odd historical tidbits, where she finds a treasure trove of inspiration. She loves photography, art, ancestry research and, of course, writing happy-ever-afters.

Books by Christina Rich

Love Inspired

A Husband for an Amish Bride
His Amish Marriage Offer
The Amish Widower's Dilemma

Love Inspired Historical

The Guardian's Promise
The Warrior's Vow
Captive on the High Seas
The Negotiated Marriage
The Marshal's Unexpected Bride
A Family for the Twins

Visit the Author Profile page at LoveInspired.com.

Lo, children are an heritage of the Lord:
and the fruit of the womb is his reward.
—*Psalm* 127:3

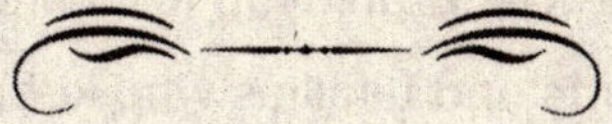

To all the educational paraprofessionals, the special education teachers, the autism specialists, the speech therapists, the behavior technicians, the personal care attendants. You matter! What you do makes a difference! Thank you for doing what you do.

To the parents and families who keep choosing,
even on those very hard days,
to love your little humans with big emotions.

Chapter One

It'd been an entire week since the last day of school. An entire week since Noah Beiler had shown up at the school to have his son evaluated for placement for the next year. Seven days of frustrating procrastination for Lydia Beachy, keeping her from doing the one thing she promised herself she would finally do before summer break was over. And yet, it'd taken this long for her to gather the courage. She knew she wouldn't be staring down Noah Beiler's drive if Mamm hadn't made the request. A request she was certain had been orchestrated by her *schwestern* too busy to bring a basket of *Mamm*'s eggs over. Lydia was even more certain Delphine had connived this plan after their last nighttime sisterly confession, when Lydia had admitted that keeping her promise to Collette had been nagging at her. Lydia didn't know when or how, but someday, even if it took her the rest of her life, she would give Delphine her just desserts.

Lydia slid her hands over the leather reins, wondering if she should turn around and go home. She could tell her sisters Noah wasn't home, but they'd know that for the untruth that it was, since he rarely left his farm anymore. Trotter, the big draft horse hitched to the buggy, bobbed his head and nickered. The horse liked to be moving. He was like the wiggly little kindergartners she worked with at the school, antsy and ready to roam the field. Forcing him to wait patiently with her indecision only fueled his nervous energy. "I know, boy," she soothed. "I need a moment."

She hadn't been to the Beilers' farm since her friend Collette had died almost four years ago. Not when tragedy had struck her own family. And afterwards, she hadn't been able to bring herself to revisit all the memories spent helping her dearest friend make a home out of the house she had moved into with Noah, the memories of helping her prepare to become a mother, watching her nurture her newborn son, all of which Lydia bore with a happy facade while jealousy seeded the root of bitterness in Lydia's heart.

But then, Collette had become ill. Lydia's bitterness had turned into guilt as she'd cared for Collette while her friend fought a losing battle with cancer. She might have been bitter at her friend for capturing the dreams Lydia had wanted for herself with Noah since the age of fourteen, a fact Collette had been fully aware of, but Lydia had never once wished her to die, especially the kind of death her friend had suffered.

Gooseflesh raced up her arms, and she shivered with the memory of those last horrific days. Collette's family had been oddly absent, but Lydia had been there, holding Collette's hand as she took her last breaths while Noah stormed from the house as if to run from grief's talons and the sadness in his *sohn*'s eyes. Jacob had been too young to understand the truth of his mother's absence, only that she'd gone, like dandelion fluff blown across the freshly cut grass. And even now, as with then, Lydia couldn't help wondering if it had all been her fault.

Trotter dug his hoof into the drive, stirring up small bits of gravel and dust. Lydia pulled in a long breath. She wasn't ready to face the subjects of a promise made. Not now, but truth be told, she'd never be ready. Although she'd lived each day with purpose and intention, there'd been moments she missed her friend, like when she'd received a job offer at the public school where she worked with children with what the *Englischers* called special needs. And Lydia definitely needed a friend now to discuss Gideon Yoder's insistence at courting her. He'd asked, and Lydia had yet to give an answer. She'd never had eyes for him, but time wasn't on her side. Gideon had always been nice enough, and had even rescued her once when her buggy had broken a wheel on the way home from a singing. He'd offered her a ride home in the rain and taken her *daed* back to help him fix the buggy on that stormy night. That had been before Noah and Collette had made their intentions known.

Close as sisters, she and Collette had planned their weddings. Lydia was supposed to marry Noah Beiler and have thirteen children, and Collette was supposed to marry Gideon Yoder. They'd both spent their teenage years lying in the cool green grass, watching the clouds while mooning over their prospective crushes. Strange how things changed. Lydia had never known about Collette's interest in Noah, and Lydia wasn't sure what had hurt her more—Collette's lack of trust to confide in her or the fact her marriage to Noah had stolen Lydia's dreams. And yet, when Collette had come to her asking for forgiveness, Lydia couldn't deny it.

Thinking about Gideon now, Lydia wasn't sure she was willing to give up her passion for working with children to become a wife, not to a man she wasn't sure she could love. Especially since Gideon had never paid attention to her until after Emmaline Miller married Uri Eicher. She had nothing against Emmaline, but Lydia deserved better than being a second choice, and Collette would have told her so, too.

And yet, the longing to have *kinner* of her own stirred deep in her heart. The need to hold a *boppli* close to her chest while gazing into the eyes of a tiny human straight from her womb was almost enough to give Gideon the answer he wanted. However, she'd lived enough life to know she could never love him, and she wasn't certain she could chase the desires of her heart for a loveless union.

Besides, before she could consider Gideon's request, she had to keep the promise she'd made to Collette all those years ago, when it was clear her friend wouldn't survive her fight. After a chance encounter with Noah and Jacob last week, she'd spilled the beans, confessing her guilt, to Delphine. Lydia couldn't put it off any longer. Her friend's child needed her, and so did Noah, whether he admitted it or not.

"Very well, Trotter," she said as she clucked and motioned for the draft horse to head up the drive. "We might as well get this over with."

The buggy rocked over the gravel, swaying Lydia back and forth. She ran over a hole in the grass-covered driveway, and an egg tumbled out of the basket. Lydia snatched it up before it fell to the floorboard and left a yolky mess. The big white house with peeling paint loomed over her like a dark shadow. The flower beds were overgrown with weeds, some nearly three feet tall. The grass needed mowing, and the clothesline repairing. It was as if the house had been forsaken, forgotten and buried along with the woman who'd so lovingly cared for it. Had Noah touched it since Collette's death?

The moment Lydia set the brake on the buggy, Noah appeared, framed by the bright red barn door. The brim of his straw hat shielded his eyes, but she could tell by the hard set of his chiseled jaw and his squared shoulders he was less than happy to see her. Jacob, with his wheat-colored curls shielded beneath his hat, clung to Noah's pant leg, as he'd done last week when she'd seen them at school. Noah stepped into the sunlight, lifting his chin, and she noticed the dark brooding clouds clinging to the hard cheekbones outlined by his dark burly beard. His brow furrowed like a torrential rainstorm, refusing to relent. And not for the first time, she noted how Jacob looked nothing like his *daed.*

Noah limped with Jacob's weight attached to him, making Noah appear much less threatening than he intended. He halted a few feet from the buggy and crossed his arms. The color of his high cheeks was more crimson than she'd imagined. Jacob, almost seven, slid to the ground and drew the tip of his finger into the dust.

"What are you doing here?" Noah's mouth pressed into a tight line as if he already knew the answer to his question. His dark eyes, so much like rich chocolate pudding with swirls of caramel vibrated with barely controlled anger.

"As I expected. No 'Hello, *gut* to see you, Lydia,'" she said, hoping to break his carved stone into a smile. She failed. Drawing in courage, Lydia descended from the buggy and grabbed the basket of eggs. She held them out for him to take, but like a statue, he didn't move. Lydia sighed and fished the handle onto her arm. "Stubborn as always, I see."

Noah's brow furrowed deep. "Stubbornness has nothing to do with your ulterior motive, Lydia."

"*Mamm* has no ulterior motives. Neither does my *daed.* He said once your new henhouse is complete, he'll bring some hens and a rooster to rebuild your flock. They are sorry about the illness that infected your birds."

He shifted his weight, and his dark broadfall pants slouched against his hips. He'd lost weight. Quite a bit, and she wondered if he was eating. She shifted her gaze to Noah's face and realized the hard lines she'd mistakenly judged as anger were most likely a side effect of eating poorly. She flicked her focus to Jacob and breathed a sigh of relief. At least the *buwe* looked well-fed. She returned her gaze to Noah. His collar rippled with the bob of his Adam's apple as he swallowed. She could tell he was uncomfortable with the subject of losing all his hens and the rooster.

"I appreciate their help, but I cannot help wondering that you coming here is not their doing," he said, staring at a spot past her shoulder. "You volunteered to try to convince me again to enroll Jacob in school."

He wasn't wrong. "Not today."

Today, her *schwestern* had volunteered her to deliver eggs. Why not kill two birds with one stone and save her the struggle of more procrastination?

He glared. "So, you plan on more visits. I told you and the teachers, Jacob does not need help. He is fine with me."

"And how do you intend to teach him next year while working the farm?" Lydia glanced at the little boy with a swath of blond bangs hanging over his eyes. Collette had pointed out how different Jacob was from other *kinner*, and had often voiced her concern to Lydia, but Lydia hadn't realized just how dissimilar Jacob was, not until she'd seen Noah and Jacob at school last week. Of course, she'd also spent the last few years working with children who needed more hands-on learning, as well as with children whose behaviors weren't always optimal. This experience made Jacob's disability more obvious to her now than when he'd been a toddler quietly keeping himself occupied. Even now, he sat in the dirt, his head tilted to the side, staring into space as if he were somewhere else than by his *daed*'s feet.

"We will get along fine." The twist of Noah's mouth showed he doubted his own words.

"How?" Lydia pleaded, her heart aching for the widower and his small *kind*, but aching even more at the fact she'd waited too long to keep good on her promise to the dearest friend she'd ever known—a friend who'd betrayed her and yet who she'd forgiven because she loved her dearly. Why had she stayed away so long?

Life. Fear. It was as simple as that, and yet, complicated by time. Shortly after Collette's death, her sister Delphine had been in a buggy accident so severe it had left her unable to walk. Lydia had helped with her sister's care, and before she knew it, Collette's request had fallen to the back of Lydia's memories. Along with Noah and Jacob. "I should have been here," she whispered.

He worked his jaw. His eyes darted to hers and then

quickly shifted away, but not before she saw the raw grief welling on red rims. "It was not your responsibility."

She reached out to touch his arm, but he pulled back. "She was my friend. Like a sister."

He bobbed his chin. "I'm sorry about Delphine."

It was her turn to change the subject. She raised the basket. "Would you like me to take the eggs inside?"

"No need. I will do it," he said, reaching his hand out for the basket. "It was good to see you, but I'm sure you have more important things to do."

She wasn't ready to give up on the *ulterior* purpose of her visit, but she could see he was as impenetrable as a cellar door during a storm. *Gotte, I need your help.*

Her mind remained silent. Not one single idea came to her about how she could convince Noah to allow her to work with his young son. She slid the wicker handle down her arm and handed it to Noah. He snagged it, the motion rocking the basket like a pendulum.

If she had thought about orchestrating what happened next, she would have, if only to prove to Noah that Jacob needed the tools she could teach him to navigate life. But she hadn't thought of dropping an egg from the basket, allowing it to break and splatter on Jacob's bare feet. The moment it did hit the ground, it splattered and a large yellow glob dripped down the child's skin. Jacob screamed, piercing Lydia's ears and tugging at her heart. He flapped the flat of his hands to his ears in rapid succession.

"Jacob!" Noah yelled as he knelt beside the boy and grabbed hold of his wrists to still his hands. "No."

The boy kicked his father's boots as he screamed. Tears streamed in pale lines through the grime coating Jacob's round cheeks. Lydia knelt beside father and son before softly touching her fingers to the child's cheek, and whispered, "Jacob."

The boy's scream stopped mid-inhale, and he flung his eyes open. She'd seen other children respond to mild events with tantrums like this, wide-eyed and wild. Some calmed easily, while others exhausted themselves before finding peace.

"I'll wipe it off." She held up the corner of her apron and then drew the fabric over the yolk. "See? All done," she said, holding her palms in the air and waving them, using one of the simple signs she'd learned recently while working with a nonverbal child at the school.

Jacob moved his mouth and uttered a grunt that sounded a lot like "Done."

Noah stood and hovered over her, watching her with concern and curiosity. Lydia smiled at him and then turned back to the boy. She nodded and repeated the sign. "Yes, *gut*, done."

Lydia straightened. Jacob tucked his small, dirt-caked hand into hers. The grimy warmth surprised her. It was like a smile engulfing her in a full-body hug. She couldn't give up on Jacob. She looked Noah in the eye with firm resolve. "Noah, I can help."

He growled. "My *sohn* doesn't need your help."

"He does. Both of you do." If only he would let her.

"We have gotten along fine so far."

"Collette used to call you her stubborn love," she said, feeling the sting of old jealous hurts. Noah flinched as if she'd slapped him, and she feared she blundered having mentioned Collette's name. "I can see she was right. Give me the summer."

"No," he said and stalked toward the stairs leading up to the porch. "Jacob, come along. Lydia has things to do."

"I do." Jacob's small voice danced toward his father as his fingers clung to her hand.

"You can't hide him away forever, Noah," she pleaded with him.

Noah turned on his heel. Beneath the brim of his straw hat his cheeks blazed with anger. "He's disruptive."

"He's a child, a gift from *Gotte*. Or have you forgotten?"

The muscles in Noah's jaw clenched, and she didn't want to wait around to hear another no from him.

"If given the chance, Jacob can learn." She moistened her lips, pressed them together and considered what she wanted to say. Noah was so guarded she didn't think he'd hear a word. However, she knew in her heart she could teach Noah how to pay attention to his son's body language and to know when he needed intervention before he escalated into a meltdown. And she just couldn't keep quiet. Before she could stop the words, they flew out of her mouth. "You can learn, too."

Everything in Noah stilled. His pulse, his thoughts, everything but the roaring in his ears. He was still working over in his mind the way Lydia had immediately brought calm to his son when he'd been trying for months without success. She didn't have to contain Jacob's arms, holding his head to keep him from hurting himself until he was done throwing a fit.

"Noah, please. He's a *gut* boy," she said, crossing her arms. Her earlier confidence waned.

"I know he's a *gut* boy," he said as he shifted his stance.

His shoulders slumped, and the tension began to drain away. "He's just different."

Sunlight illuminated her green eyes. The lavender of her dress highlighted the color even more. Her white-blond hair was neatly pinned beneath her cap, but she looked like the same unruly young girl he'd been friends with most of his life. He'd always liked it when she wore shades of purple. When she'd first stepped out of the buggy with her basket, he'd struggled to find his breath, and then he'd had to battle the self-deprecation at noticing how pretty she was when the woman he had married was gone from this Earth.

"Different, *jah*," she said. "And, if I could guess, capable of doing more than either of us could ever imagine. He is smart, Noah. I can see his intelligence, but you have to allow him space to grow."

Noah almost scoffed, but the look on Lydia's face told him she believed what she said, and she wasn't just being nice to get her way. He wanted to believe her, but he couldn't afford to buy into her disillusions. She hadn't been here seeing to Jacob's needs day in and day out for the last few years. He had, and he knew just how little his *sohn* accomplished in a day. How little he'd allowed him to accomplish. His *sohn* had grown in stature, but his mind hadn't developed. The list of things Jacob couldn't do far outweighed the things he could. And that was something Noah knew as fact.

Noah shifted the basket on his arm, careful not to dislodge another egg and risk Jacob tumbling into another tantrum. Although the previous one had been short-lived, thanks to Lydia Beachy.

How many nights had he lain in bed, praying for help

with the child, not of his blood but of his heart? Those prayers often turned into tantrums of his own. He didn't fault *Gotte* for taking Collette from him and Jacob. He was even grateful that Collette hadn't suffered long, but he did fault *Gotte* for leaving Noah and Jacob without a lamp to light their way. If Noah had known Collette would die, leaving him to care for her child, a child belonging to another man, would he have done things differently? Would he have still offered Collette a solution to her dire predicament and married her? Yes, he would have married Collette. He knew in his heart he would have made the same choices. He just needed some help. The two times he'd sought help from an elder within the community, he'd walked away feeling more defeated than hopeful. The rod would not fix his son. And no matter how many times he tried to explain Jacob's disability, the elders' solution was still the same, a switch to his bare bottom. Noah cringed.

Noah wanted help, and she was right, he needed it, but accepting assistance from Lydia was not a wise decision on his part.

"Noah," Lydia said in that quiet and calm way of hers that he recalled so well from the days she sat with Collette during her illness. "I'm not saying I can fix him. His autism will not go away. It will be with Jacob all his life, but given time, he can teach us how to listen to him, and in turn, we can teach him how to manage his days."

"I don't know, Lydia," he said, gazing down at the child still clinging to Lydia's hand. His son owned his heart, and he wanted the best for him, but when he thought of the future, he drew a blank. All he saw were days of tantrums and unintelligible mutterings. He saw his child following him around the farm like a lost little lamb, never working beside him as he plowed the fields. "What you did a moment ago was *gut, jah*? But it was one time. What about tomorrow, next week, next year? You can't be with us all the time. You have work, and your family."

The sun shone down on her face, making her smile seem more brilliant than it was. Hope illuminated her green eyes, tempting him to grasp hold of her offer. "The good news is, school is out for the summer, which means my days are free."

"I can't, Lydia." He didn't want to be beholden to her, or to anyone, for that matter.

"Noah," she said. "Who keeps Jacob while you work the fields and care for the animals?"

"I haven't worked the fields in two years. Other than that, he stays with me." He moistened his dry lips. The days were long, and very little got done, but they managed. Except, they didn't. And now he needed to burn the old chicken coops and rebuild if he was going to fulfill customer orders, but he didn't have time, and he guessed he was too stubborn to ask for help.

Or worse, too ashamed to invite anyone into his life for fear they would judge him as a terrible father if Jacob fell into one of his tantrums. Just like the elders had judged him.

Was Lydia the answer to his prayers?

"Give me the summer, Noah," she pleaded.

He shifted his weight as he chewed on the inside of his cheek. "Two weeks." That was the time he needed to get his farm somewhat back in order.

Her shoulders sank. "That's not enough time."

"It's what I'm willing to give you." Any more than that and he might start longing for fellowship with the community again—with her. And he couldn't subject Jacob to ridicule, even if it was only behind closed doors.

She released a heavy sigh. "Four."

He started to argue but she held up her free hand.

"But, if you see changes in Jacob, you give me more time."

"No. This is a bad idea. We will be fine," he said, reaching out to take Jacob's hand. His son dug his heels into the dirt and grunted as he clawed at Lydia's arm. "You should go."

"No go. No go," Jacob cried as he stomped his feet.

"Noah, please."

Lydia's soft whisper threatened to implode his resolve to stand firm. The plea watering in her eyes had him shifting his gaze to the lone redbud Collette had planted the fall they moved into their home. Its budding flowers had long gone now that summer knocked on their door.

"I can help."

"No," he said, shaking his head. He hooked an arm around his kicking son and held him tight against his side to keep from dropping him. "Goodbye, Lydia. Give your *mamm* my thanks."

Without a backward glance, he marched up the stairs, careful to hold on to Jacob in his tantrum without falling down. He flung open the screen door and disappeared into the shadows of his home. He deposited the basket on the table and then took Jacob to the safe corner, where Noah had covered the walls and floor with cushions, soft blankets and plush pillows to keep Jacob from harming himself whenever he flailed around. Assured Jacob was secure in the safe corner, Noah crept back to the kitchen window and watched as Lydia navigated the buggy onto the road.

A part of him wanted to call her back, so much so his muscles vibrated with exertion as he clung to the counter. He would not chase after her and beg for her time. Jacob's piercing screams gave way to a deep, keening moan. The voice in Noah's head echoed the emotions spilling from his *sohn*, but he kept them there, locked in the confines of his mind, even though the desire to relent and give in to all the frustrations that had built up to an unwavering crescendo through his late wife's diagnosis, her death and Jacob's difficult upraising pressed against his chest.

The black buggy slowly ascended the hill and then disappeared, with no hint of its existence outside the mark left on his memory. Drawing in a ragged breath, he swept off his hat and tossed it onto the counter before fisting his fingers into his hair. He tugged on the strands to feel something other than the anguish tearing him apart inside. A roar of anger knotted in his throat, but he choked it down and collapsed onto the floor. He spread his palms out beside him. The ceramic tiles Collette had chosen when they built the home cooled his calluses.

"I don't want to be angry, *Gotte*. I don't, but I don't know how else to be. Maybe if I didn't feel like such a failure..."

Then what?

He'd failed his son by not getting help to his late wife quickly enough when she went into labor, and he couldn't help but feel as if he'd failed her, too. He couldn't save her from the cancer that had ravished her body, and he couldn't save his son.

"*Gotte*," he muttered through clenched teeth. "This lot

is more than I can endure, but what choice do I have? It is mine to bear."

He couldn't roll back time and ignore the stirrings in his heart when he'd offered marriage to Collette to save her from disgrace. He couldn't go back and make his buggy race faster down the ride to the phone booth to call for help when her labor pains became too much. No matter how many times he'd replayed the scenario in his head. Nothing changed. It always ended up with his son fighting for his life and coming out with battle scars he didn't ask for or deserve. And Collette gone from this Earth. If he'd known what the future held for them, for him… No, he would have done it all the same if only to keep Collette from being banned from the community. Still, he just couldn't help wondering what his life would have been like if he wouldn't have done what a *gut* friend should. Maybe he would have peace in his heart.

Jacob moaned from the other room, and Noah knew that thought was not true, because he would have always wondered what had happened to Collette. Not marrying her wouldn't have stopped her from a difficult labor, and it certainly wouldn't have kept the cancer away. As difficult as days with his son were, Jacob filled a place in his heart he'd never imagined could be true. He wouldn't change Jacob's presence in his life for anything. Still, if only his child was…like other *kinner*.

He knocked the back of his head against the cabinet and allowed the despised tears to flow down his cheeks. "*Gotte*, dare I ask why? No, I can't. I won't. I cannot see what is ahead of me, but you can."

Somehow, he had to find a way to trust *Gotte*'s will. Even if it meant he and Jacob never left home.

It'd been *Gotte*'s will to bless him and Collette with a child through a difficult childbirth. He recalled Collette's grateful tears as they visited their new *boppli* in the neonatal intensive care unit. The outlook for Jacob's life had been grim. The lack of oxygen during birth had done its damage, but their baby had lived.

Noah ground his teeth together. Jacob had autism on top of the intellectual disability. Had that too been *Gotte*'s will?

If only Collette hadn't died, then they could have managed Jacob together. She'd been a soft and gentle woman. With her demeanor, she would have been able to tame Jacob's outbursts, or so he'd believed. Now he wasn't certain, but at least he could have managed the farm better with help. As it was, he couldn't tear down the chicken coops and burn them without fear of endangering Jacob, which meant rebuilding his flock and supplying eggs to his customers was impossible. Elam Beachy's offer to help rebuild his flock was no good with Jacob underfoot.

Noah stretched his legs out in front of him and noticed the silence. Looking around the corner to check on Jacob, he saw his son looking at him. Even though he barely spoke beyond unintelligible muttering, Noah saw the question etched on his *sohn*'s brow. Noah nodded and patted his thigh. "Come."

Jacob crawled across the floor on his hands and knees and then climbed onto his lap. Noah curled his arms around his son and buried his face into the boy's soft locks, the same shade of blond as Collette's had been. "*Ich lieba dich.*"

His heart beat for his child, more than he ever thought possible. He wanted the best for him. He wanted to teach him how to plow the fields, raise chickens, to cook and clean for himself. To love without conditions, as Collette had loved him, even though she knew the truth, that his heart had belonged to Lydia. He wanted to teach Jacob to live a *gut* life. But to do that, they needed community. Their community. And that didn't seem attainable unless he used the rod.

It'd been more than two years since Noah had pulled back and introverted himself and Jacob to their home. Helpless. Lonely. He'd done all he could to ignore the sideways glances whenever they gathered together as a community, even though he wanted to run and hide. The final blow had come when Susan Mueller, the bishop's wife, suggested he let someone better suited care for Jacob, like Collette's *mamm*, one of her *schwestern* or one of his. Someone who'd give the boy *proper guidance*, with the rod if necessary. Anyone but him.

Even now, anger at Susan's suggestion seethed in his veins. He wouldn't send his child away. Unknowingly to the bishop's wife, Collette's family would never take Jacob. They wouldn't even see him unless by accident, and if in public, they'd pretend he was well loved by them. Sensing, and maybe wrongly so, that Susan Mueller spoke for the *gmay*, Noah had slipped from the community, isolating them from everything but family dinners held every other Sunday at his *mamm*'s house. To keep from being a burden, he'd only accepted help from his *mamm* and *schwestern* once a week so he could run errands and deliver eggs before the illness had taken over his birds. His *daed* had always remained silent whenever they were around, but that was *Daed*. Although, Noah wished he'd say something to ease the thought he'd somehow disappointed him.

"Oh, *sohn*, what are we going to do?"

Noah needed help. He knew that. He'd prayed for help. Prayed in tears and desperation. But when he'd taken his son to the school, armed with paperwork from the child psychiatrist and doctors they'd seen the week prior, the enthusiasm and optimism at Jacob's appearance had scared Noah. He'd prepared himself for condemnation and disapproval. He'd even readied himself for the suggestion he send his son away. The team of teachers and social workers sitting around the short round table had been genuinely happy to see Jacob. Instead of rushing in the opposite direction, or looking at him with disapproval, the team—Lydia included—had exuded hope and confidence for Jacob, something he'd lost a long time ago. Their words, their plan of action, had teased Noah into wanting to believe. But, like a leech, the years-long struggle of trying to understand his son and find their place in this world had sucked the hope right out of him.

He smoothed the wheat-colored locks from Jacob's brow and kissed his forehead. He wanted to grab hold of what the school offered, but experiencing hope deferred for so long, he was too scared to take a step.

Inviting Lydia into their lives, even for two weeks, meant inviting the community back in. The thought of their speculation, well intended, but misplaced advice, as well as the community running from the awkwardness of Jacob scared Noah. It was easier to isolate himself and Jacob than to be isolated by the community. And he didn't know if that was fear talking or his pride. He didn't care if anyone thought badly of him as a single *daed*. He'd already failed Collette as a husband, but he didn't relish the idea anyone might think badly of his son. Noah didn't want Jacob to be rejected. Not for any reason, especially because they thought he was a wicked child. He wasn't. He was sweet. Until he wasn't. And usually because he grew frustrated when he couldn't communicate what he wanted to say, and he wasn't understood when he tried.

Lydia's words pressed hard into his thoughts. He looked down at his son. His small chest rose and fell in an even, calm cadence, his eyes closed. Was Lydia right? Could Jacob teach him to listen? Had he gotten it wrong all this time trying to be the teacher when he should have been the student?

He didn't know. He'd have to set aside his pride and ask for Lydia's help, which was easy enough. Setting aside his fear of disappointment was another story, and that was something he wasn't sure he could do.

Chapter Two

Her sisters' laughter raced out of the screen door faster than their bare feet clattering down the wooden ramp. Lydia's sister Delphine, nearing twenty, burst through the door last. Flour coated her *kapp*, face and upper body. She made a show of pumping the wheels of her chair as she chased after the younger *kinner*, her wheels clattering down the ramp and her smile more brilliant than the morning sun. "I'm going to get you."

The girls ran across the grass and hid behind Lydia. "Don't trample the flowers," Lydia scolded.

"But Lydia," Alice, her eight-year-old sister, squealed. "Delphine is going to run me over."

"No, she won't," Bridget, the ten-year-old, said. "She only said that."

Jessie, almost thirteen, crossed her arms and scowled. "She put a frog in our bed."

"And you thought it would be good form to get back at her?" Lydia said.

"Technically, I didn't put a frog in your bed" Delphine said. Her dark eyebrows lifted in feigned innocence as she slowly navigated her wheelchair over the grass. Her sister had done well adjusting to life after the accident that took her ability to walk. And not for one moment had she allowed the accident to steal her joy and tendency to prank her siblings, at least not since she moved past the initial pain of her injuries. She'd even forgiven Jared Stoltzfus for causing her paralysis, proving Delphine was a much better Amish woman than Lydia was, although Lydia had forgiven Collette for stealing Noah. However, Lydia knew the two situations were as far apart as over-easy eggs and charred eggs. At least Collette hadn't robbed her of her mobility.

"That's beside the point," Jessie argued. "Bribing Silas with his favorite cookies to do your dirty work is the same as you putting the frog in our bed."

"Gracious," Lydia said as she jabbed the garden spade into the ground and then stood up. "No wonder *Mamm* is exhausted all the time. How does she keep up with all of you? Not to mention Silas, Isaiah, Remmy, Pauly and *Daed*. Never mind. The three of you," she said, motioning to the three younger girls. "Go clean up the mess before *Mamm* and *Daed* return from Butterfly Gardens. And you," she said, turning toward Delphine. "Finish the laundry, then make lunch. All our brothers will be in from the fields soon."

"My cookies," Delphine said.

"Bridget will finish them until the clothes are ready to be put away."

The three younger sisters stalked toward the house, but not without giving Delphine their final shots. Alice stuck out her tongue. Bridget scowled, and Jessie grabbed hold of Delphine's *kapp* and tugged, leaving some of the bobby pins loose and the *kapp* askew. "You're lucky I don't push you to the end of the drive and leave you there."

"Jessie," Lydia warned. "Go inside now. And there will be no more frogs in beds."

Jessie snorted. "We'll see about that. I don't have to bribe my brothers to do my dirty work. So you better watch your bed, Delphine."

Lydia straightened Delphine's *kapp* and replaced the pins, then stood back to wipe the perspiration from her brow. "You would think you're a child and not a grown woman, Del. Can't you leave them alone?"

Delphine laughed. "What fun would that be? Besides, they started it."

Lydia rolled her eyes. "Highly unlikely. If I remember, you oversalted the meal Jessie made for the church brunch on Sunday. You embarrassed her in front of everyone, especially her latest crush, Samuel Mueller."

"She put vinegar in my water."

Lydia pinched the bridge of her nose. "I suppose I'm wasting air asking you to put a stop to the pranks."

"Probably," Delphine said. "But on a more serious note, you've been overly testy and contemplative lately. Ever since school has been out. Wondering if it is Gideon or Noah."

Her sister wasn't always one to get straight to the point. She knew Lydia's worries about Jacob, Noah, and the promise she had yet to keep to Collette. This was just Delphine's way of getting information. "Just trying to adjust to a new schedule," Lydia said.

"No. I don't think that's it. What's wrong? Did Gideon change his mind?"

Lydia shifted to her knees and began focusing on digging holes for the flowers *Mamm* would bring back from the greenhouse, so her perceptive sister wouldn't see more than she should. "No. I didn't give him an answer."

"Why not?" Delphine asked, and then quickly said, "Oh, Noah Beiler."

Lydia swiveled to look at her sister and shielded her eyes from the sun. "What is that supposed to mean?"

Her sister shrugged, but it didn't remove the smug look from her face. "You delivered eggs to him last week. And that seems to be when your happy, cheery self disappeared."

"I delivered eggs. No thanks to you and our *schwestern*, making yourselves oddly too busy for a neighborly outing." She thrust the spade into the ground and cut a circle before digging her fingers into the warm dirt. "Nothing more, nothing less."

"We got done what you've been avoiding since school was out." Delphine's blush had little to do with the afternoon sun. "How was he?"

"Who?" Lydia asked, wishing her sister would leave the topic alone. She had been thinking about her visit to Noah's house, and how much she wanted to help Jacob. She'd been in the meeting at the school and knew the challenges, but she'd faced tougher ones and accomplished what needed to be done for the best possible outcome. There were still meltdowns and challenges with some of the children, but most times those incidents were few and far between, and on a manageable level.

"Noah, silly. And his *sohn*, Jacob. It's been months since they've been to church."

Lydia sighed and then sat on the ground. She pulled her knees to her chest and wriggled her bare toes in the soft grass. "Stubborn."

Laughter spilled from Delphine, easing some of the tension from Lydia's shoulders. "Did you expect anything less? Collette always said he refused to ask for help until after disaster struck."

It was Lydia's turn to laugh. "She did, didn't she? I miss her."

"I do, too, Lydia. She was a good friend, even though she stole Noah from you."

"We can't help who the heart wants, can we? It just would have been nice if she had let me know how she felt. Anyway, I wish I had been as good of a friend," Lydia said, trying to keep the ache in her heart from spilling down her cheeks.

"What do you mean, Lydia? You helped care for her and Jacob when she was sick, so Noah could work the fields."

"It never felt like enough, Del."

"You gave all you had to give." Her *schwester* leaned back against her chair. Her all-knowing gaze assessed her with the same shrewdness their mother often used.

"Not all. You know that," Lydia said, feeling the guilt more today than she had yesterday, or even last week. "I should have looked after Noah and Jacob like Collette asked and made sure they were okay, much sooner than today."

"That wasn't fair of her, Lydia. Surely you know that," she said. "Did she expect you to marry Noah and become Jacob's mother?"

Delphine's words gave her pause. Her *schwester* often spoke without thought. Still, she couldn't help wondering if that was exactly what Collette had intended with her request. Which is why Lydia had pushed Noah and Jacob to the back of her mind all this time. It didn't seem fair of her to step into the life her friend could no longer live, even if Collette had ripped it from her to begin with. No, that wasn't true. Noah had never declared his emotions or feelings to Lydia, but he had to Collette. Which meant Noah had never been hers in the first place.

"It doesn't matter. I made a promise, and I've failed to keep it all this time." Not that she wanted to marry Noah. Not now. Not when she'd always be his second choice. Just like Gideon's. Marriage was the furthest thing from her mind. She only wanted to work with Jacob and learn from him and then help Noah understand his son better while relaying some of the things she'd attained while working with special-needs children at the school. "At first, I thought to give Noah his space, and then days passed, weeks and years. And now he won't let me in. I don't think he'll let anyone in, and I can't help wondering if I'd only kept my promise shortly after Collette's death things would be different."

"You can't carry that, Lydia."

And yet she did, especially after seeing how much Jacob and Noah needed intervention. "I do. Jacob doesn't speak and Noah seems lost. When he showed up at the school two weeks ago, I had hoped… Maybe he was ready, but he seems adamant that the only answer is to keep them both isolated to their farm."

"Well, Lydia," Delphine said, "if I know you, you won't let that happen. You wouldn't let me keep to myself after the accident."

"You're my sister, Del."

"And you've taken it upon yourself to carry the burden

of a little boy and his father on behalf of a woman who was your best friend."

"I offered help last week. Noah sent me away." His rejection hurt more than she expected, and she wasn't sure why. At first, she'd thought the despair she felt as she left his house had to do with Jacob's wails, but contemplating the scenario in her head the last few days, she wondered if it was the anguish in Noah's eyes when he'd told her goodbye, as if he thought he'd never see her again. She'd seen that look when they'd sat across from each other and held Collette's hands while they listened to the doctor explain that medical intervention was no longer an option for Collette. Seeing the pain and desolation, she'd wanted to swoop in and fix things for Noah. Then, just as now, he'd shut her out, and she'd let him.

"Keep pressing until he sees the light, Lydia. Just as you did with me."

Lydia kept quiet, contemplating her sister's words.

"Look, if there is one thing I know, it's that you're as stubborn as Noah Beiler." Delphine leaned forward and reached out to touch Lydia's shoulder until she glanced up at her. Delphine squeezed and then settled back in her chair. "You're not a quitter. You never have been, and you've never allowed anyone you care about to quit either. That's who you are. It's your gift. So I say, keep offering until Noah relents."

Buggy wheels crunched up their drive before Lydia could find a reason to deny her sister's wisdom. *Daed* pulled the buggy to a halt, jumped down, and then reached a hand up to *Mamm*. "Your mother nearly bought every flower in stock."

"Oh, Elam," *Mamm* said, nudging her father's shoulder

with hers. "The flowers can wait. First, we have news. Lydia, your *daed* is going to round up the boys after lunch, and all of you are going to the Beilers'."

"Which Beilers, *Mamm*?" Lydia's pulse thundered in her ears. She knew the answer before she asked.

"Noah and Jacob, of course," *Mamm* said.

"Your *mamm* insisted we drop flowers off at Noah's, and while we were there, she told him we'd be by after lunch to help tear down the coops and get them burned. He can't sell eggs if he doesn't have chickens, and he can't have chickens if he doesn't have a place to keep them. And I," her father said, "cannot argue with sound wisdom."

"And you want Lydia to help tear down the coops?" Delphine asked, one eyebrow arched high in a teasing salute. Lydia was tempted to wheel her ornery sister to the end of the drive, just like Jessie had threatened.

"No, of course not." *Mamm*'s brow furrowed as her gaze traveled from Delphine's head to her knees. "She'll keep watch over Jacob while the men do the work," *Mamm* said.

Lydia circled her hand toward Delphine. "Frogs and sisterly love in the form of retribution."

Mamm nodded in understanding. "Delphine, you're lucky it was only flour. One of these days you'll wake up with honey in your hair."

Lydia giggled. "Don't give them any ideas. Noah asked for help?" Curiosity burned in Lydia. Had Noah decided she could have the summer with Jacob?

"Not exactly," *Daed* said as he glanced lovingly at his wife. The hope budding in Lydia's chest deflated like a popped balloon. "Your *mamm* orchestrated the entire thing. Somehow I have a free afternoon today, if your brothers did as they were told while we were out, and so do they. She told Noah without question a crew would be by this afternoon, and you would keep Jacob. Your *mamm* didn't even give the poor man the opportunity to say no."

"I see," Lydia said, picking herself off the ground.

As if her sister read her thoughts, Delphine said, "Any opportunity to intervene is worth taking, right? Like *Mamm*, don't take no for an answer."

"What's all this about?" *Mamm* asked.

Lydia stilled her sister's interference with a warning glare. She didn't want her parents to know about the promise she'd made and failed to keep. "Only that I offered to work with Jacob over the summer."

"Is that a *gut* idea, Lydia?" *Daed* asked. "Two unmarried people spending so much time together? My daughter?"

Her pulse skipped a beat. "It's not like that, *Daed*. I'm sure Noah wouldn't be present. I just want to use the tools I've learned while working at the school to teach Jacob to communicate, and maybe lessen his tendency to escalate into tantrums."

"I don't know, Lydia," *Mamm* said. "That's a lot of time at Noah's home."

"*Mamm*," Delphine said. "Lydia only wants to help Noah's *sohn*, so he and Jacob won't feel so isolated from the community. You would do the same."

Bless her sister for stating the obvious and standing up for what she knew Lydia wanted in her heart: to keep her promise.

"She has you there," *Daed* said. "But your *mamm* is married. However, I'll agree on two conditions."

Lydia was almost afraid to ask, but at this point, she'd

do just about anything to get the chance to help Noah and Jacob. "What conditions, *Daed*?"

"First, you'll take your sisters. They'll help keep speculation away."

"Okay, but you must understand, I'll have to introduce them slowly. One at a time until Jacob becomes used to them."

"I can agree to that."

"And the other condition?"

"Noah has to agree."

Listening for a hint of noise from his napping son, Noah paced the front porch as he waited for Elam Beachy and his sons to arrive. However, his nervousness had nothing to do with Elam and Lydia's brothers, but with Lydia. She'd been the focus of his thoughts since he'd watched her drive away last week. And for more reasons than he cared to consider.

He'd kept his fear close, shielding himself from the hope she'd offered. He would have maintained his resolve if Lydia's parents hadn't arrived after one of Jacob's tantrums. Exhausted and vulnerable, Noah had taken hold of the offer Lydia's parents gave him without hesitation, and he hoped he wouldn't regret it when Lydia asked once again if she could work with Jacob for the summer.

She would. He knew she would. He couldn't have her so close, not when she tempted him to reach outside of his circumstances and court her. He held secrets that weren't his to divulge, and he wouldn't entertain thoughts of courtship when he couldn't be truthful about his marriage and Jacob's paternity. He removed his hat and ran his fingers through his hair. He'd have to find his resolve against his better judgment and once again tell her no. That was a conversation he didn't want to have.

The rumble of a tractor signaled Elam's arrival. He shielded his eyes against the sun and waited until the stack on the tractor peeked over the hill. He released the breath he'd been holding and sneaked into the house to check on Jacob. His son slept soundly on the cushions, and anxiousness vibrated through Noah at not having his son to shield him from Lydia and her family.

The tractor murmured to a stop. Noah eased the screen door open, stepped out onto the porch, and waved to Elam. Noah tucked his thumbs into his suspenders and descended the steps as the buggy rolled to a stop behind the tractor. Isaiah stepped down from the buggy, and Noah half hoped Lydia had stayed at home and one of her sisters had come instead. But the moment she climbed from the buggy, with her light blue dress, white apron and wide green eyes, unexpected relief washed over him. He almost felt a twinge of expectation within his chest, as if one of the bands that had held him so tightly for the last few years had broken, releasing one tiny piece of the tension keeping him captive.

Not good. Not good at all. Rolling his shoulders, Noah shook off the sensation, attempting to free himself, and strolled toward Elam. "*Denki* for coming."

"*Jah*, we're glad to help," Elam said. "Like Malinda said, we had a free afternoon, and it's always *gut* to keep our hands from idleness."

"Noah." Isaiah, one of Lydia's *bruders*, stuck out his hand. "*Gut* to see you again."

"*Jah*, *denki*," Noah said as he shook his hand. "Remmy, Pauly and Silas."

"Hello, Noah," Lydia said as she stepped forward, as if he'd forgotten about her.

How could he when she'd been the main focus of his thoughts for the last week?

"Lydia." He shifted his weight and glanced at his boots. "Jacob is napping inside." He turned toward her father, and said, "Shall we?"

"Noah," Lydia said, forcing his attention back to her. "Is there anything I should know?"

He tilted his head, confused by her question.

"Will he want a snack when he wakes up? Will he become anxious if he doesn't see you?"

Those were questions he didn't have answers to. "I, uh, don't know."

Her mouth formed an O. She nodded. "All right, I guess I'll find out."

Noah ground his teeth together.

"I'm not judging you, Noah," she said. "I thought it would be an easier transition for Jacob if I knew his likes and dislikes."

"It's not that I don't know. It's just been us, and Jacob doesn't talk."

"We understand, *sohn*," Elam said, and Noah had a sense that Lydia's father was trying to keep the peace between them. "Lydia and Jacob will be fine. Let's get those coops down."

Noah watched Lydia until she disappeared into the house, and then dressed in the protective clothing he had purchased a month ago when it became obvious his chickens were sick.

Two hours later, after shoving their outer garments into trash bags and scrubbing their skin, Noah, Elam and

Lydia's brothers stood back and stared at the two large piles of wood and screen. "Tonight, when the air cools and the wind dies down, I'll burn."

"Is that safe with Jacob being unattended?" Elam asked.

What choice did he have? "I'll wait until he's asleep."

"I'll stay," Isaiah said. "It'll be better that way in case the fire gets out of hand. Two are better than one, *jah*?"

"*Denki*," Noah said. He didn't want to be a burden or have anyone go out of their way for him. They'd already done enough. "I'm sure you have better things to do."

"No," Elam said. "Isaiah is right. We'll come back after dinner. It'll be cool enough and still light. Lydia can stay with Jacob again."

Noah looked toward the *haus*, thankful it remained intact and that he didn't hear his son's hollers echoing in his ears. "How do you think they fared?"

"My *dochder* is capable," Elam said. "It's what she does."

"I didn't mean to suggest she wasn't, but I know my son." Pride pulled his shoulders back and he waited for Elam to speak badly of Jacob.

"And she knows children." Elam turned and walked toward the house. Noah lengthened his stride to catch up and heard Lydia's brothers behind them. Noah swallowed the knot in his throat and considered the fact that Elam hadn't called Jacob out for the troubled child he was, but simply called him a child.

"I haven't had the opportunity to be around many children that weren't my own," Noah said.

"Lydia has every day," Elam said. "You know chickens and the fields. You know the weather by the clouds and the rising and setting of the sun. Lydia knows children. She has a way with them, even the toughest ones, as I think you fear your son might be. He's not a lost cause, you know."

Noah inhaled and exhaled, wishing to be anywhere but here. Longing to have any conversation but this one.

"Have you heard of horse whisperers?"

"I have, but have never met one," Noah said, wondering what horse whisperers had to do with Lydia and his son.

"I believe my daughter is one, only with children." Elam stopped walking and turned toward Noah. "Before we came out here, Delphine told me Lydia offered to work with Jacob over the summer."

"I told her no."

"I know, and I'm not telling you what to do, Noah, but if you want to give your *sohn* a good fighting chance, you should let those who can and are willing to help, help. If nothing else, an hour or two a day won't hurt Jacob and will allow you much needed time to get work done around the farm."

He shoved the bubbling hope down to keep it from overcoming him, but considered the truth in Elam's words. "I don't know, Elam."

Noah walked up the stairs and stopped in his tracks at an unfamiliar sound teasing his ears through the screen door. He bent his head and listened. A child's laughter mingled with Lydia's singsong voice. Noah eased the door open, careful to keep it from squeaking, and tip-toed through the kitchen and into the living room.

Lydia held Jacob's hands playing patty-cake. She smacked his hands together and rolled them around as she sang the catchy tune. She rocked her head from side to side as she swayed toward Jacob and then gently tickled him.

Noah's breath caught in his chest and his knees quaked as he witnessed the sound of laughter coinciding with unfiltered, authentic joy on his *buwe*'s face. For the first time since his wife's death, Noah felt something more than trudging through the days. And for the first time in his son's young life, he heard something other than unintelligible utterings and uncontrolled tantrums. His heart yearned to move across the floor and join the pair, but his feet were heavy, rooted like pilings ten feet in the ground bound with cement. In shock? Surprise? Joy? Grief? He didn't know. All his days with Jacob were nothing more than highs and lows between raging silence and Jacob's furious meltdowns.

The spark of hope Lydia had offered him last week ignited, blazing a trail in every cell of his body. Elam's words about Lydia's abilities were like a banner of stars hanging over his head, and he knew right then and there he had to give her a chance. He had to give her a chance for Jacob. He just hoped he didn't regret his decision at the end of summer.

Chapter Three

A soft knock startled Lydia, and she dropped Jacob's hands as she looked over her shoulder. Noah watched her from the edge of the dining room with his arms crossed. His gaze was steady and assessing, as if he'd never seen her before. His nostrils flared and the beard cloaking his jaw rolled like waves as if he was trying to control emotions he didn't want to face. She'd always thought he was handsome, with his dark hair and eyes, even when they were in school, long before he married her best friend. But now, seeing him fight so hard to hold on to the threads binding him to his despair, she found him even more handsome. Her heartstrings reached toward him, and she had the urge to offer him a strength she didn't know she had.

She'd felt the same two weeks ago at school when he'd walked the halls holding Jacob's hand. He'd held his head high with purpose, but years of hopelessness had veiled his eyes. Then, just as now, she'd wanted to embrace him, if only to carry his burden for a few seconds. Two weeks ago, the motive watering the garden of her heart was fertilized out of guilt for failing to keep her promise to Collette. Now she wasn't sure guilt was the only factor as her sister's words played in the background of her mind. Had her friend intended for her to take her place as Noah's wife and Jacob's mother? She hoped not, because that was one promise she couldn't keep.

As if he'd read her mind, his eyes grew wide, and he quickly shifted his gaze to Jacob before falling back to her. She shuddered at the raw emotion framed by the crow's-feet at the corners of his eyes.

"Lydia," her *daed* called from outside, breaking the thread between them.

"You can come in, Elam," Noah said, not taking his eyes from hers.

Jacob jumped onto her lap and gripped her cheeks with his little fingers, turning her face toward him. "T-t-t," he uttered.

Lydia covered his hands with hers and held them against her cheeks. Pressing her lips together, she said "Mmmmmmore."

The child released her and sat on the floor. "Mmm—mmm."

"*Gut*, Jacob."

The child clapped his hands together, smiling as he did so.

"We will come back after dinner as planned," her father said, pulling her attention away from Jacob. "But it is time to go."

"We're coming back?" she asked, standing and self-consciously smoothing the wrinkles from her dress. Jacob tugged on her skirts, uttering noises. She held her finger to her mouth and then took his hand in hers. "Patience, Jacob."

"Yes," Noah said, eyeing her cautiously. "After the temperatures cool, if you're willing to watch Jacob, you'll come back with your father and *bruders* so we can burn the debris."

"Of course I'll watch him," Lydia said, smiling down at Jacob. "We've become friends."

"And tomorrow," her father said, "we'll come back first thing in the morning to scout out new places far from the previous ones to build coops."

Noah uncrossed his arms and let them fall to his side. "Elam, you don't have to do that."

"No, I don't, but I want to," her *daed* said.

"Blessing each other is our way," Lydia said. "It's what we do for each other. Just as we gather to raise a barn for one of our neighbors, my *daed* and *bruders* will help build the coops, and I will entertain Jacob. He is such a joy and able."

She knelt beside Jacob and held her hand in front of him. He laid his small hand in hers. "*Denki*, Jacob. I have to go home now, but I will come again, *jah*?"

The boy pressed his mouth together, and Lydia braced herself for a tantrum, and that was the last thing she wanted to happen in front of Noah if she hoped to convince him to give her more than just today. "Remember, Jacob, watch me," she said, pointing to herself. "Deep breath in. Deep breath out. Do you want me to come back?"

"Mmm—mmm." He tapped the tips of his fingers together in the sign she'd shown him earlier.

The smile filling his chubby cheeks honored her. "*Jah*, when I come back, we will play more patty-cake." She repeated the sign for *more* and then clapped her hands together.

He fidgeted in front of her for a few seconds, nodded

his head and then ran to the cushioned area where his toys were.

"I'll bring dinner when we return," she said.

"No," Noah said. His harsh tone wasn't meant to bite. She knew that by the way he sank into his shoulders. "We have leftovers and Elam said after dinner."

"Jacob needs more than peanut butter and jelly sandwiches," she said. "Not that I meant to pry, but he wanted a snack, and it wasn't hard to notice you're running short on supplies."

"I can take care of my *sohn*," he said.

She didn't mean to offend him, but now that she heard her words play back in her thoughts she could understand how he could take them badly.

"I'm sure my daughter didn't mean it that way, did you, Lydia?" *Daed* said this with a mixture of disbelief and humor.

"I'm sure she did, Elam," Noah said. "As I remember, she's never been one to keep her tongue when something is on her mind."

Except now, she held her tongue. There was so much she wanted to say and ask, but all she could think about was whether Noah would allow her to come back tonight.

"Elam, do you mind if I speak with Lydia a moment before you leave?" Noah asked.

Without hesitation, her father called out to Jacob, and once he had the child's attention, held his hand out to him. "Would you like to see the tractor?"

Jacob nodded and raced across the room to take her father's hand. He skipped beside her *daed* as they went outside.

Lydia worried her hands together, afraid Noah was

about to reprimand her for interfering, which would lead to him reminding her that he never agreed to let her work with Jacob. He was about to put a solid wall between her and the promise she intended to keep to his late wife.

"What you've done, in the short time with him," Noah said. "I'm impressed."

"*Denki*," she said, folding her hands together.

"He won't remember tomorrow."

"You don't know that," she said, releasing her fingers and pulling her shoulders back, ready to defend Jacob's intelligence. "He's smart."

"He's…Jacob."

She wondered what he really meant to say, what he thought of his son. "He's a child with limited abilities, but he's still capable. You have to give him a chance."

His jaw clenched and anger rose high in his cheeks. He took a few breaths. "I'm with him every day, Lydia. I know my *sohn*. I know his limitations."

She shook her head. "No. You only know Jacob through the lens of your own limitations and perceptions."

He flinched. "You hold nothing back, do you?"

"Not when it comes to children—especially not when it comes to children like Jacob."

He moistened his lips, shifted his weight and looked around the room as if to find an object to focus on, as if to seek something outside this room. His gaze settled on his feet. "What do you mean I know my son through my own lens?"

"You don't have the tools needed to help Jacob succeed, not yet. But I would like to help. Both of you."

Noah leaned against the wall as if he was too weary to hold himself up anymore. "I don't know what to expect, or if I should expect anything, but I'm willing to give you a chance."

"Denki."

"For Jacob," he said. "And Lydia?"

"Yes?"

"I'm giving you two hours a day for two weeks. That's it," he said. "Monday through Friday. No Saturdays or Sundays."

Her heart swelled with joy at the opportunity. Two weeks were better than nothing, even though Noah took those two weeks and turned them into ten days. It wasn't a lot. "I understand."

She nearly squealed in excitement. She couldn't wait to prove to Noah what she could do, and even more, she couldn't wait to prove to him what his son could do.

Time flew faster than Noah imagined, but then he expected Lydia, her *daed* and her *bruders* to arrive after dinnertime. Much to his surprise, two buggies and the tractor arrived well before it was time to eat. Panic struck him when all the Beachy *kinner* spilled from the two buggies along with Malinda and Elam Beachy. Glancing at the door, he calculated his chances of closing it and sweeping Jacob upstairs to hide before anyone noticed. These were his walls, his sanctuary, and he wanted to hide just as he had done for far too long.

This Beachy invasion forced his pulse to race, and he didn't like it. He rarely had visitors, and never more than a few at a time. Their home was Jacob's place to be himself, and Noah never knew if too many visitors at a time would cause his son to have a tantrum.

Lydia must have considered this. The boys unloaded

tables from the truck-bed trailer Elam pulled behind the tractor. Malinda and Lydia's *schwestern* covered them with tablecloths and laid out a feast.

The object of his constant thoughts strolled across the yard. He pulled back into the shadows but kept her in his sight as she walked up the stairs. She knocked on the screen door. "Hello."

Air rushed out of his lungs. Closing his eyes, he hung his head.

"Noah," Lydia called. "We've brought food. Lots of food."

His stomach grumbled.

"Mmm—mmm," Jacob squealed as his bare feet clattered over the kitchen tiles. Noah swept his son into his arms and hugged him close. His child's excitement at hearing Lydia's voice eased his anxiousness. "*Jah*, Lydia is here."

He pushed open the screen door and stepped into the evening sunlight. "Hi."

"Hi," she said.

Jacob lurched from his arms toward Lydia. She caught Jacob, but she stumbled toward the stairs with the force. The heel of her foot hung over the tread and she flailed. Grabbing her by the waist with both of his arms, Noah pulled her and Jacob to safety.

Her eyes grew wide, but then she laughed. "That was close."

Too close. She could have been hurt; so could Jacob. He looked down at her heart-shaped face, searching for any hint of fear. "Are you all right?"

"Yes, of course."

He released her waist and immediately missed the feeling of her. Stepping back, he chastised himself for thinking about Lydia as a woman and not as his late wife's closest friend. Once *his* closest friend. There'd been a time, before Collette, that he'd wanted to court Lydia. He'd almost asked her to go on a buggy ride after one of their singings when they were youth, but Gideon Yoder had beat him to it, or so he'd heard. By the time he'd cooled his rejection enough, he'd discovered Collette's trouble and convinced Collette to marry him instead.

"Are you hungry, Jacob?" Lydia asked his son as she put him down him on his feet. "Come."

She took Jacob's hand and skipped down the stairs as if she hadn't almost tumbled down them with his son in her arms. Of course it hadn't been her fault, but Jacob's enthusiasm at seeing Lydia. An enthusiasm that not only warmed Noah's but mirrored the excitement in his heart,

Lydia glanced over her shoulder. "Are you coming? *Mamm* made fried chicken and potato salad, and Jessie made chocolate cake."

Forgetting the hard days of the recent past, Noah followed close on her heels.

"And what did you make?" he teased, unwarranted. He searched for the walls he'd kept in place and couldn't find them. Even when he and Jacob went to his parents' for dinner, he'd kept up walls. But with Lydia, they disintegrated.

Noah had said Lydia would only be here for an hour or two a day to work with Jacob, but he was already regretting his decision, and they hadn't even begun the two weeks.

She slowed her strides, allowing him to walk alongside her. "Shoofly pie."

His favorite. Did she remember from when they were children, or had she guessed? "Breakfast for dinner?"

"Only if you want it. You can save it for breakfast, too."

"I think I'll have it for both."

She burst into laughter as she swung Jacob onto a bench seat. "You'll have to fight my *bruders* and *schwestern* for it."

"Now that's not fair," he said, sitting beside Jacob. "I'm completely outnumbered."

Lydia slid a paper plate from the stack and gave him a teasing smile as she picked up one of the pie plates and settled it on the paper plate before setting it in front of him. "With me on your side, you can't lose."

His heart skipped a beat and refused to settle as he watched her spoon a small bit of shoofly pie onto another paper plate. Using a pair of tongs, she dug around for a chicken leg and scooped some potato salad to the side. She set the plate in front of Jacob. She'd come to his house to champion his difficult child, and she fought hard for that place. He glanced down at the plate in front of him, an entire pie. His favorite. Breakfast for dinner, minus a small scoop for Jacob, sat in front of him. Now she was proving she would champion him, too. But was it only for this moment, or would she continue to do so? Dare he hope?

The sound of buggy wheels met his ears. He stood up and tried to glance around the other vehicles. "Who could that be?"

No sooner had he asked than a tall blond Amish man climbed down from the buggy, and Noah's hopes plummeted, crashing like a vulnerable tree in a windstorm. It seemed Gideon Yoder had been invited to dinner, too.

Chapter Four

Lydia couldn't believe her eyes, but she could believe the pit in her stomach. For a short moment, the walls she'd carefully kept in place for many years, ever since Collette and Noah announced to the community they would marry, had disappeared. And the thicker walls Noah had built with his grief over Collette's death and Jacob's tough upbringing had lost all substance. For a moment, the clock had turned backward. It'd been like they were friends again, laughing and smiling, before he'd married Collette, leaving Lydia heartbroken and confused.

"Hello," Gideon said as he perused her. "I thought I might find you here."

The skin on her brow pinched as the source of her irritation the past few weeks spoke to her. "Why is that?"

"Trudy Smucker."

She glanced at Noah, who was twirling his fork above the shoofly pie she'd made for him. *Get it together, Lydia.* The pie hadn't been intended solely for him. Not at first. She had made it because she knew it was his favorite or at least had been. She just hadn't intended on giving all the pie to Noah, but the easy teasing between them had her dropping the entire pie on his plate. Seemed now he'd lost his appetite. As had she.

Thanks to Trudy Smucker's good intentions, the once-tantalizing flavors of *Mamm*'s fried chicken—which had teased Lydia's senses the entire ride to Noah's, reminding her she hadn't eaten today—left her stomach sour.

"Trudy?" *Mamm* asked. "Where'd you cross her?"

"At the phone shanty. *Daed* had me order some exotic wood for an *Englischer*'s custom desk. He's slowing down a bit and letting me take over more of the business. Told Trudy I was heading over to take you for a ride, Lydia."

Lydia rolled her eyes at Gideon's knowing look. "I wish you wouldn't have."

Bless Trudy. She meant well by her unintended gossip. Lydia knew that. Young, Trudy often allowed her tongue to get away from her before her thoughts caught up, especially when a bachelor was in her presence. Which was how Gideon had come to be here right now. She didn't blame Trudy, as she'd been her age once and wanted to impress a single Amish man, but Lydia wished the girl wouldn't unknowingly encourage Gideon's pursuit. It wasn't that Lydia didn't like him, but she didn't appreciate his recent dogged chase of her, or the way he acted as if she should be grateful for his attention.

"Why not?" Gideon asked.

"It insinuates we're courting." Lydia certainly didn't like the way he made his intentions known to Trudy Smucker. Because now the entire community would think they were courting. Lydia massaged the back of her neck as she considered how to counter any gossip that might come out of Gideon's interaction with Trudy when a thought came to her. Had Gideon told Trudy his view on how Lydia was nearing the precipice of being too old to bear children, as he'd so boldly told her? She widened her eyes and then narrowed them. If word got around the community, would everyone start playing matchmaker and making their opinions known on Lydia's singleness? And poor Trudy, three years younger, must be beside herself thinking she was chasing time, too. She made a mental note to have a heart-to-heart with Trudy about the dangers of bowing to peer pressure.

"You're not courting?" Noah asked.

Gideon shrugged.

"No," Lydia said, and couldn't help noticing the way Noah's shoulders relaxed. "We are not, and now I'll have to explain that to Trudy." Hopefully she wasn't as hard headed asGideon's was.

"Trudy stopped by with a pie this afternoon," *Mamm* said. "You can take the plate back tomorrow."

Gritting her teeth, Lydia kept her tongue from reminding *Mamm* about sharing anything with Trudy Smucker.

"Lydia has another commitment this evening," *Daed* said to Gideon. "You're welcome to share the meal with us."

Lydia sensed Noah's discomfort return. He'd kept to himself for so long, she imagined he was less than pleased having the entire Beachy family arrive on his front lawn, and even more so with Gideon's arrival. She was thankful for her father speaking up on her behalf, although she was certain his main goal was helping her hold her tongue so she wouldn't give wind to the rant she'd confided to her parents the last time Gideon had showed up unannounced and demanded a ride. Which, she might add, had been the fifth time she'd told him no. Somehow, she'd been able to convince him to help with evening chores, giving her *bruders* a much-needed break after the storm cleanup, and then told him kindly she wasn't interested in riding in his open buggy.

"Trudy mentioned the plans to burn the old coops," Gideon said as he grabbed a paper plate from the stack. "I'm happy to help an old friend and then drive Lydia home. If Noah is agreeable."

If *Noah* was agreeable? She balled her fists. Agreeable to Gideon's help or taking her home when the burning was done? Her father's hand clasped her shoulder, and she released her nails from her palms.

"I can't speak for Lydia, but I don't mind the help," Noah said, his voice low and hard, and if she heard right, a little shaky. She risked a glance at Noah, but he stared at his fork, which somehow annoyed her because she couldn't see his eyes and read his thoughts.

"*Denki*, Gideon, but the day's been long, and I'd prefer to go home with my parents," Lydia said.

Daed dropped his hand from her shoulder and made his way between *Mamm* and Alice. "I'm starved and my beautiful *fraa* and daughters have prepared a *wunderbar* meal. Let's eat."

Lydia glanced around Noah's farm for an easy excuse to make her escape, but that would make her a coward. She'd just have to find a firmer way to tell Gideon she was not interested in taking rides with him, for any reason. Obviously, telling him *no* the last several times hadn't been enough. She breathed and shook the tension from her fingers.

If she was a *gut* Amish woman, she'd serve Gideon just as she had Noah, but a fire of independence rose in her unlike any she'd felt except while advocating for the children she worked with at the school. She slid onto the bench next to Jacob, and dished him another scoop of potato salad, careful not to touch them to any other food items on his plate.

Gideon took a seat across from Noah at the picnic table and shoved his empty plate toward Lydia. "It's *gut* to see you, Noah. We've missed you at church."

There was something in Gideon's voice that presented a challenge as he thrust his plate farther into her view, as if she hadn't noticed his silent demand. A low guttural growl vibrated across the bench and Lydia felt like she was watching two billy goats about to butt heads.

"I've been busy," Noah said, without looking away from the food on his fork.

Lydia plopped a spoonful of potatoes onto Gideon's plate a little harder than she should have, nearly causing him to drop it onto the table.

Her father cleared his throat. "Let's not be remiss in giving thanks. Shall we?"

Lydia bowed her head, and closing her eyes, she waited in silence for her *daed* to say amen. Jacob stirred beside her and made a soft groan. She touched two fingers to the top of his hand. The child jerked his hand away, causing his fork to jab Lydia's palm. She hissed instead of crying aloud, but *Daed*'s hasty amen had her lifting her head. A quick glance around, and she knew the sound hadn't gone unnoticed, especially by Noah.

She rubbed her palm against her thigh to soothe the ache. Noah's leg bumped against the table, drawing her attention. His brow furrowed deep, and she understood the silent question, but not wanting to draw attention to them and make Noah any more uncomfortable than he already was, she reached across the table for the potato salad.

Jacob tapped the tips of his fingers together. "Mmm—mmm."

Euphoria filled her, but the audience of one sitting across the picnic table kept her from praising Noah's *sohn* even with a *gut job*, which he needed to hear more than the man sitting beside Jacob needed to preserve his pride. However, she couldn't bring herself to acknowledge Jacob's success at his quick learning.

"Your *sohn* doesn't speak?"

Noah tensed, and Lydia bit the inside of her cheek to keep from telling Gideon the child was none of his concern. The silence between them drowned out the birds and her siblings' chatter. Noah laid his fork down and ruffled Jacob's wavy wheat-colored hair.

"Jacob has a developmental disability, but he is a quick learner, and—" he smiled at her "—Lydia has done wonders with him. *Denki*."

It didn't seem possible under the heat of the evening sun, but her cheeks warmed several degrees at his compliment. *Jah*, she'd heard thanks before and been told she'd done a *gut* job, but the fact Noah recognized today's accomplishment meant a lot to her. "Of course. I have found while working with children at the school that we don't often give them enough credit." Her cheeks grew warmer at Noah's intense gaze. "They are smart and capable. We just have to give them tools to use, and then we adjust as we need."

The clearing of Gideon's throat drew her attention. Once she looked at him, he offered her a twisted grin. "He's six, *jah*?"

Noah nodded. "Almost seven."

"If he hasn't learned to speak by now, Lydia," Gideon said, "what makes you think he will ever learn?"

Lydia lifted her cup of lemonade to her mouth and sipped as she thought about how to appropriately answer him without sounding rude or making Jacob appear less than. Because he wasn't. He was more, and different, but fully capable.

"There's more to communication than speaking, Gideon," Alice, her brilliant eight-year-old sister, said from down the table. "Isn't that right, Lyd? You've told me that bunches of times when I tried talking to Daniel Lambright at church. He doesn't talk much, either."

Lydia nodded. Daniel was her friend Naomi's youngest brother, and about the same age as Jacob. She tilted her head and considered Jacob for a moment. Would the two boys get along? Would Jacob allow another little boy into his world? A plan began to form in her head, but she filed it away, making a mental reminder to ask Naomi her thoughts about them playing together before she approached Noah on the subject.

"You're right, Alice," Lydia said. "There's more to communicating than speaking. And once we learn Jacob's language, we'll all do just fine. Isn't that right, Jacob?"

The little boy grinned up at her. Grease from *Mamm*'s fried chicken outlined the corners of his mouth, and he had a small bit of potato salad on his nose, but she found him endearing and she couldn't wait to get to know him more. To see if he took after her friend Collette, serene and peaceful, like a quiet sunny day with barely a cloud in the sky, or if he'd be like his *daed*, a silent brooder and grouchy. Given his eyes were bright with joy and contentment, she hoped he was more like his *mamm*. She wasn't certain she'd have the patience to deal with two Noah Beilers.

* * *

Noah sent up a prayer of thanks when Elam declared dinner was *gut* and he was ready to burn the chicken coops. It gave him permission to quit pushing his shoofly pie around with his fork. He disliked disappointing Lydia since she'd made the pie for him, but with Gideon's observant gaze, Noah didn't want to draw attention to himself.

He pushed himself off the bench and shook the crumbs from Jacob's feast off his pants leg. "*Denki* for the meal. It was *gut* and much appreciated."

"We should have done this much sooner," Malinda said. "Collette was like another Beachy running underfoot, and you were like family, too, Noah. I don't know how we let so much time get away from us like we did."

"A lot has happened." Uncomfortable with thoughts of Collette and Delphine and all their families had lost in the last few years, he tucked his thumbs around his suspenders and shifted. At least Lydia's sister had survived the accident. He wasn't sure he would have hoped for Collette's life to continue longer than it had. The cancer had devoured her. Although he missed her at times, he was content she no longer suffered as she had, and even more content their son had never had to witness the worst of her illness.

"Well," Gideon said. "Should we get to burning the coops?"

Grateful Gideon had changed the subject, Noah nearly shook the man's hand. If the conversation had continued to wander toward the past, he didn't know that he'd be able to keep the mist from cloaking his eyes. "*Jah*, it's good to start."

"I'll grab the tractor so we can move the wood piles

away from the house and barn." Noah turned toward the barn, but Jacob had somehow scrambled down from the picnic bench and locked himself onto Noah's leg. He swept his *sohn* into his arm. "I'm going to help burn the chicken *haus*, okay?"

Jacob smacked his palms against his ears and violently shook his head.

"Jacob," he said, his voice hard, stern. He saw Lydia shaking her head over his son's shoulder, and he clenched his jaw. Heat burned the tips of his ears, and he was beginning to regret allowing the Beachy family to invade his home. He didn't like feeling chastised by anyone about anything, especially when it came to his *sohn*. He would have told her so, too, if Jacob hadn't started kicking his legs and then pulled his wet-noodle act, where his entire body fell limp, forcing Noah to do what he could to keep from dropping the child.

Lydia closed the distance between them and helped him support Jacob until he was safely on the ground. That was when he saw Gideon's jaw slacken in shock only moments before he turned toward the picnic table and began helping clear the food.

Noah moistened his lips and dropped his chin to his chest. He'd done well keeping his home from judgment. Until today. Today, it all fell apart, and something shattered deep in his chest.

"Noah, I'm sorry," Lydia whispered. "I shouldn't have done that, not in front of everyone, but reacting to Jacob only causes him to react even more. You have to trust he is able to respond to your calmness."

He lifted his head and glared. "I don't mean to be

rude, but I would appreciate it if you took your family and Gideon away from here."

She shook her head, defiant and wild as he'd remembered her from the days before he'd married Collette. "We're here to help, and we're not leaving until the job is done."

Jacob's tantrum escalated, and Noah's shoulders tensed.

"When we're done, we'll leave, and if you choose to hide yourself and Jacob away from the world, then so be it, but you'll only cause more harm to the *kind* than good."

She knelt beside Jacob and touched her fingers to his cheek, just as she'd done earlier. Noah watched in amazement as his *sohn* froze in mid-motion and opened his eyes, revealing the glaze of rage.

Holding her hands up, palms facing out, she wiggled them. "Done?"

Noah heard the question inflected in her tone. Jacob lifted his torso from the ground, curled his feet beneath him and mimicked Lydia as his fit ground to an abrupt halt.

"Are you ready?" Gideon asked. "Elam and the boys are grabbing the diesel can and tying rags to the end of the limbs. It shouldn't take any time to burn the coops."

How many times had he helped his own *daed* burn brush piles with diesel soaked rags? Preparing the small branches as fire starters was something he should have done already. It was something he should have thought about, but hadn't.

Drawing in a ragged breath, Noah looked from Gideon to Lydia, then to his tantrum-prone child, and shook his head.

"He'll be fine, Noah," Gideon said. "She'll be fine, too, and I think we both know her well enough to know she doesn't back down when she's set her mind to doing something. Isn't that right, Lydia?"

It was a little over an hour ago he'd been irritated at Gideon for showing up uninvited. Now he was thankful. They'd been friends once, before Gideon had taken Lydia on a buggy ride all those years ago, leaving Noah with little choice to help Collette before she had been completely disgraced and banned from the community. And although Noah didn't think they'd ever be good friends again, it was nice to have someone else's voice in his head besides his own. Even if that someone seemed to be intent on courting Lydia. Not that it mattered. It wasn't like he planned on courting her.

Even though he still experienced some of those old feelings he'd once held for Lydia.

"The Lydia I knew in school wouldn't back down, but I don't know this Lydia," he said, hoping to solidify in his mind that he didn't care if Gideon courted the woman Noah once wanted to marry. However, he regretted his words once he saw disappointment pucker her perfectly pink lips.

"Trust me, Noah," Gideon said. "She hasn't changed. If anything, she's grown more obstinate with age."

Jumping to her feet, Lydia fisted her hands and snorted. Noah sensed a storm brewing, especially if her heightened color was any indication.

"You act like you know me, Gideon." Lydia crossed her arms. "You don't. You mistake my passion for obstinance, and when it comes to children who need some extra assistance to succeed in life, I'll stand my ground.

Fiercely." She flicked a fiery gaze toward him, and a shiver of dread raced down Noah's spine. "Even against stubborn parents, if it's for the good of the child."

"I don't know how I got wrapped up in your ire," Noah said. "I wasn't the one who called you obstinate."

"No, you didn't have to. It was plain as day with your half-turned smirk that you agreed with Gideon," she said.

Had he done that? Smirked? He'd have to be more careful to guard his reactions while he was around people. It wouldn't do him or Jacob any good if everyone tried to read his intentions, especially where Lydia was concerned. Again, it wasn't as if he had any intentions with her. He didn't. He couldn't. Losing the *fraa Gotte* had so obviously chosen for him to cancer had been bad enough. He wouldn't survive the loss of a woman he'd once held with deep affection, and possibly still did, if he was going to be honest with himself.

"Fine," he said, and turned to walk toward the barn and his tractor. He didn't invite Gideon to follow, but he heard the man's boots shuffling against the grass and knew he followed close behind him.

"I suppose you'll need a mask to cover your face while we burn," Noah said, willing Gideon to give him some distance. He wished his thoughts would, too, but he kept thinking about Lydia. Strong, capable, independent Lydia who was never afraid to back down from a fight.

"If you have an extra, and don't mind," Gideon said.

"*Jah.*" *Jah*, he had an extra. He clenched his jaw and chastised himself for the sarcasm bounding around in his head. He'd grown grumpy in his singleness. Collette had had a way of placating him, but she had been soft…gentle, almost timid at times, submissive to even his smallest suggestions, so much so he felt guilty for requesting lemonade instead of iced tea for dinner. His *mamm* reminded him a *gut* Amish woman was submissive to her husband, but Noah couldn't help wondering if his *mamm* understood his concerns about his late *fraa*. Like a chameleon, her character seemed to disappear and meld into his. Lydia never would have allowed her opinions to be quieted like Collette had.

He'd chosen Collette because she'd needed a husband and quickly, and Gideon had taken Lydia for a ride in his buggy, and when young Noah had compared himself to athletic Gideon, why would Lydia have ever chosen him? Not when he'd seen the comradery between Lydia and Gideon, the way they had teased and joked around with each other. Of course, Lydia had teased Noah, too. Thinking back on those old days, was it possible Lydia had looked at him the way he'd seen her look at Gideon? It didn't matter, because he had decided his best course of action was to be a good friend to Collette, by becoming her *mann* and her *boppli*'s *daed*. Especially since he'd believed Lydia had set her intentions on Gideon by taking a public buggy ride. Noah also decided Collette's joyful outlook on life and the way she got lost in perusing flowers or watching butterflies was something he needed in his life. He had chosen her because she was Collette, as far from Lydia as possible, and he didn't think he'd ever have to worry about having his heart crushed, until she'd died.

"Of course, I don't mind carrying the debris to the burn spot."

Noah's brow creased as he stepped into the cool shadow of the barn and turned toward Gideon. "What?"

"If you aren't hooking the truck bed to the tractor, and

have extra pair of gloves, too, I can carry the boards to where we're burning them."

"I appreciate the offer," Noah said, relaxing now that his thoughts were on the task at hand and far from his late wife and her best friend. He motioned for Gideon to follow. He grabbed a box of protective masks from the workbench and some gloves. "Considering the nature of the task at hand, we'll need to gear up. I don't think Lydia would forgive me if you or her family developed bird flu while helping me."

"You overestimate Lydia's affection for me." Gideon laughed.

"Lydia is a compassionate woman. She wouldn't want anyone to suffer illness."

Gideon clamped a hand on Noah's shoulder. "And here I thought you didn't know Lydia."

Noah pulled away from Gideon. "I don't."

Not anymore.

"Neither do I, my friend," Gideon said. "I think I missed my chance with her, not realizing just what kind of woman Lydia is soon enough."

Noah had the sense of being sucker punched in the chest. Air caught in his lungs and an uncomfortable pressure filled him. He didn't need to ask Gideon what kind of woman Lydia was. She was one of a kind. Maybe not the sort his *mamm* considered a *gut* Amish woman, but Noah knew her worth and value, not only as a friend, but as a woman. The kind of woman who remained by her best friend's side through long, hard days when her husband couldn't, because he was too much of a coward to face death. The kind of woman who took care of a toddler while his *mamm* lay dying.

Noah had loved Collette, but not with the same intensity he thought he could love Lydia. Which was his cross to carry. If he'd only loved his wife more, maybe *Gotte* would have spared her the suffering of disease, and he and his *sohn* the pain of grief. He feared Collette's death had been his punishment for not valuing her or loving her as he should. And that was a secret he'd take to his own grave.

"I am surprised you and Lydia never married," Noah found himself saying.

Choked laughter rumbled from Gideon. "Like I said, if only I'd known what kind of woman Lydia was much sooner, instead of licking my wounds after you married Collette, and then chasing Emmaline." Gideon shrugged. "I think Lydia and I make sense now. There are very few of us single Amish men available, but I don't think she feels the same."

Confusion bunched Noah's brow. "I see," he said, except he didn't. "I'm sorry about Collette. It just kind of happened."

"I know. I understand," Gideon said. "Uri said the same thing about Emmaline. Funny, I always thought you had a thing for Lydia. You two were inseparable, except when she was with Collette."

Had he had it all wrong? Had he misjudged the situation between Gideon and Lydia all those years ago? Would it have mattered given his knowledge of Collette's situation? "Shall we catch up with Elam and the boys?" Noah asked, hoping the busyness of his hands would keep his mind off Lydia and the what ifs of the past.

Chapter Five

"Jacob, look," Lydia said as she pulled the two hourglasses from her oversize bag holding all the tools she thought she might need during the two-hour session. The short time Noah allowed her wasn't what she needed to be successful with Jacob, but she'd take what she could get and pray he would allow longer sessions as he saw his *sohn*'s improvement.

Jacob blinked his little eyes. He jumped up and, walking on the balls of his feet, scrambled toward her. He reached for the hourglass, but Lydia pulled the object back.

She heard a hard scoff from behind her when Jacob tossed his hands in the air, let them fall to his side in fists and began to growl.

"Patience, Jacob," she said as she placed the flat of her palm against her chest and made circular motions. "Please."

"N-no!" Jacob dropped onto the floor.

"I don't think—"

Lydia pressed her palm toward Noah, quieting him. If she was going to make any headway with Jacob, she couldn't allow his *daed* to interfere. And now that he'd given his reluctant permission, she wasn't going to miss the opportunity. Even if he'd only given her ten days.

"Jacob, say please," she said as she repeated the motion, this time holding the hourglass toward him. He reached to take it, but she repeated the word and action. He had the look of a child on the verge of a tantrum. She silently prayed he wouldn't. Especially since his father stood behind them, watching, and no doubt brooding. The tension knotting her neck drained the moment Jacob's shoulders drooped. *Victory!* Small and short-lived, for sure and for certain, but it was a victory nonetheless and she'd take it.

Making a fist, he turned it sideways and tapped his chest. "P-please."

Lydia smiled, and handed him the smaller hourglass, and sat the other one on the table. "Very *gut*, Jacob. When this one is done, I have more surprises in my bag."

She unfolded her crossed legs and stood up, leaving Jacob to be entertained by the sand falling from one side to the other as he flipped it upside down. She was very aware she had less than five minutes to convince Noah to quit hovering like a mother hen. Folding her hands in front of her, she walked toward him. He shifted away from the counter and took a step back as she approached.

"What?" he asked.

"You have given me two weeks to work with Jacob," she said. "Ten days to be exact. Two hours each day."

He smirked, the same smirk he'd given a few days before when Gideon had called her obstinate. It irritated her, and yet that half-cocked twitch was alarmingly...adorable. It reminded her of when they were *kinner* and he didn't think she could run as fast as the boys or climb a tree near as well. Once she had climbed higher and won a peanut butter sandwich for her efforts, then broken her arm when she fell as she climbed down.

"And?"

"You, Noah Beiler," she said, poking her finger into his muscular chest, "are interfering with my time."

He stepped back again and rubbed the spot she'd jabbed. "Overseeing your work with my *sohn* is not interfering."

"No?" She arched an eyebrow and clenched her fists to keep from poking him again. "When you interrupt the conversation I'm having with Jacob with your wealth of experience, you're interfering."

He snorted.

She crossed her arms and glared.

"What conversation? You're the only one making any words with clarity and you talk to him as if he understands what you're saying."

"Of course I do. How is he going to learn if he isn't taught, Noah?" Lydia blew out a breath, causing her shoulders to sag. She shook her head. Disappointment at Noah's lack of faith in her raged against the excitement of the opportunity. She sighed again. "And didn't you hear and see him respond? There is more to conversation than speaking. As I told you last week, I need to learn Jacob's language. He needs to learn mine. We are getting to know each other. Your doubts in him will only cause him to falter."

Just as Noah's doubts in her were creeping into her confidence. Maybe she couldn't teach Jacob? But if she couldn't, it wasn't because he wasn't capable, but because she wasn't. She rubbed her lips together and swallowed the doubt. She could do this. She'd worked with verbally challenged children for the last few years. Jacob was no different. Except he was. But only because of the promise she'd made to Collette.

"Your huffing and puffing and shifting weight does neither of us any good. The noise distracts us." She would be successful with Jacob, for Jacob—and for Noah. She had to. There was no room for failure. "He needs to know we believe in him. Not just me, but you too, Noah."

"I believe in him," he said.

"No, you love him, and you want to protect him." Just like he had protected her when the lowest branch she had clung to that day had snapped before she jumped to her feet. All their friends had run home scared they'd get in trouble. Not Noah. He had hovered above her, waiting for her to cry, and then helped her to her feet, careful not to jar her broken arm. He'd walked her home that day, straight to her *daed*, all the while telling her it was okay for her to cry. He'd been a hero that day. Her hero. And seeing him protect his *sohn* the way he had protected her only made those memories sharper in her mind. "You don't believe Jacob is capable. Not yet, but you will. Now, if you would kindly leave the *haus* and send my sister in, we have work to do. As do you. My father is here to help build coops, not do them alone while you hover."

Fire ignited in his eyes, just as she had intended, but the chord thrumming in her chest had been unexpected. She massaged the discomfort with her fingers. Why had his annoyance at her chastisement caused such a reaction from her? Because she was capturing glimpses of the man she'd dreamed of marrying. The compassionate, caring man. The man who protected those around him and did what was right. If she could convince him that allowing her to work with Jacob was the right thing to do, would he grant her more time? Or would he remain the man who took up challenges and didn't let anyone help him fight his battles? "I shouldn't have spoken so harshly. I'm sorry. I know you don't intend to slack off while my *daed* and *bruders* do the work. That was not my intention."

He dipped his chin as if to acknowledge her apology and then lifted his gaze to hold hers for a moment. "No need to apologize, Lydia. You told the truth. We both have jobs to do today. I guess I should be getting on with mine, and let you do yours."

"You are a *gut* man, Noah, and a *wunderbar* father. And a *gut* friend," she said, recalling the tenderness with which he had treated her while walking her home the day she'd fallen from the tree. The old blush of a first crush crashed against her, and she once again felt like she was thirteen, chasing after Noah Beiler just to catch a glimpse of his beautiful smile.

"*Denki.* Although I haven't been a friend to anyone for a long time. As for being a *gut daed*—I don't know." He glanced at his child. Noah looked lost and confused and broken. Lydia felt the stirrings of his pain, and wanted to fix it for him, but she knew her abilities were limited to the progress Noah would allow himself to see.

"You are a *gut daed*," she said, reaching out to touch his forearm. "But you have to believe in your *sohn*."

He turned his anguish-filled gaze to her, and she wanted to pull him into a hug and tell him everything would be well. Instead, she dropped her hand from him and shook the emotions away. She stiffened her weak knees.

Gracious, she had to ignore the stirrings thrumming against her heartstrings, though. She was here for one reason, and one reason only. Work with Jacob, not court his *daed.*

She glanced over her shoulder and took notice of how much sand was left in the hourglass on the table before it emptied the top side. The sand was more than it should be, meaning Jacob had touched it, which was okay. Today was only about introduction. She turned back to Noah. "If you can't believe in him, I'm not sure how much success we'll have, but allowing me to work with him, well, that's a start."

"I will leave you then," he said, turning from her, but not before she witnessed the shadow of doubt clinging to him. He grabbed his hat from the hook by the door and slipped out the screen door.

"Please, Noah, I need you to believe in him," she whispered under her breath. The fact that he'd quit hovering and left was a sliver of hope.

Lydia watched him walk across the porch, his head hanging low, but she didn't think he was hurt by her words. She was certain he was thinking about what she'd said. At least she hoped so. Turning toward Jacob, she felt her heart swell with warmth, just as it did every time she worked with a child who was termed developmentally delayed or disabled. She wished everyone saw what she saw: intelligence, kindness, authenticity and love in action, even though many of the children she worked with didn't quite understand what love really was.

She laughed at herself. Hadn't she told Noah he didn't give Jacob enough credit? And here she was doing the same. How did she know what Jacob understood or didn't understand about love? She didn't.

"Jacob, are you ready for another surprise?"

He flipped the hourglass upside down.

"Jacob?" She sat on the floor beside him and touched the hand holding the timer. "Would you like the next surprise?"

He pulled his hand back and growled.

"Please," she said as she signed to him. "Use your words."

She pulled a set of magnetic shapes from her bag and showed him how they worked. Jacob launched toward her, but she pulled back and held out her other hand for the hourglass. He pressed his lips together and kicked his feet.

The tension in Noah's muscles pulled taut, like the blade on a band saw, ready to snap at his *sohn*'s screams chasing him down the stairs. He forced his feet to keep moving, one step in front of the other. Lydia had asked him to trust her. No, she hadn't asked him to trust her, she'd asked him to believe in Jacob. Right now, he believed Jacob might cause Lydia harm, but since she was adamant about him not interfering, he kept walking, praying she wouldn't get hurt during his *sohn*'s tantrum.

It took all his self-control to not ask her to leave. He didn't like his faults pointed out, but she was right. Elam and Lydia's *bruders* were here to help him build the chicken coops, not complete the buildings by themselves. Even though he'd been skeptical, he'd also been so taken with how enthralled Jacob was with Lydia. The look in his *sohn*'s eyes had the same giddy, glossy sheen that Noah sensed took over his eyes too whenever Lydia was around.

He hadn't been *hovering*, as she called it. He hadn't been huffing and puffing, either. He wasn't sure what he'd been doing, but it had nothing to do with displeasure with Lydia and everything to do with his amazement of her and how she'd got Jacob to refocus his tantrum and talk with his hands.

"Bridget," he hollered at the miniature version of Lydia poking her hand through the fence to pet a doe-eyed milk goat.

She turned and waved, and he waved back for her to come toward him, but she didn't leave the goat. What was wrong with the Beachy women? None of them seem to respond to a man's request, especially Lydia. How dare she kick him out of his own house?

He stopped beside Bridget. "Your sister is asking for you."

"They don't have ears."

"Who doesn't have ears?"

"Your goats, silly," she said, laughing. "Why don't they have ears? How can they hear?"

"They have ears," Noah said, pointing at the side of Gloria's head. "See? They're just smaller. They're called Lamancha goats. Good for their milk. Have you tasted goat's milk before?"

"Ew," she said.

"It's good." He laughed. "Just ask Jacob. He loves goat's milk."

"He can't talk," she responded.

He felt like he'd been hit in the gut. Hadn't he just had a similar conversation with Lydia? "Sure he can. You ask

Jacob if he likes goat's milk and see what happens. But wait until your sister tells you it's okay."

He wouldn't want Bridget getting reprimanded for interrupting like he had.

"Okay," she said.

"And after we're done building the coops and Lydia is done working with Jacob, I'll show you how to milk a goat if you'd like."

The child squealed and clapped her hands, startling Gloria. "I've milked our cow, but not our goats. That'll be fun."

"Off with you then, but be sure to listen to Lydia."

He watched her skip toward the house as he made his way toward Elam, and he couldn't help thinking how he'd offered Bridget a reward once she completed the task Lydia had for her. It wasn't any different than Lydia offering Jacob a reward for doing what she asked, like saying please. Maybe he'd misjudged her abilities to teach his son. He'd gone into their agreement expecting her to fail. He nearly laughed. Lydia didn't fail. At least she hadn't when they were kids. She'd always been up to a challenge, and when he or one of his friends told her she couldn't do something, she always proved them wrong. He remembered one time she even beat Gideon in a buggy race. The fear pounding in his veins as he had watched her take off renewed its course right now. He'd tried talking her out of it, but Gideon had goaded her on. Then all their friends had, too. It wasn't long after that he'd been told about Gideon taking Lydia on a buggy ride, and why wouldn't Gideon have asked her? Even in Noah's fear, Lydia had been glorious in her race, not only beautiful, but amazing in the way she had handled the reins. It had been then and there he'd thought he loved her, but then he'd heard the rumors, and hadn't had it in his heart to confront his friends about the truth, so he'd given up on the idea of courting her.

Now, part of him couldn't help hoping her dogged tenacity and competitiveness would disappear so he and Jacob could get back to their quiet lives. The other part of him wanted her to succeed. Even though his guard had been up a few nights ago when Gideon arrived, he was beginning to realize how much he'd missed being around the community. Lydia was making him realize how much he'd missed talking with another adult, which he was certain had to be the reason he was so taken with her. Maybe if he allowed others in, he wouldn't be so hungry for conversation with her.

"I was beginning to wonder if you'd show up," Elam said as Noah neared the pad they'd marked out for the first structure.

"I probably wouldn't have if Lydia hadn't kicked me out of my house."

Elam laughed. "Sounds like Lydia."

"Can't say I was fond of being bossed around."

"I don't blame you," Elam said as he wiped perspiration from his brow. "All the years Lydia's worked at the school, I've never seen her in action until last week. I've met some of the teachers she's worked with, and they all have spoken highly of her and have encouraged her to go to a school to teach."

This information surprised Noah. Would Lydia defy the *Ordnung*? Would she leave the community to chase an *Englicher*'s job?

"She won't. She's said as much, but I have to tell you,

Noah, I wouldn't blame her if she did. I can see the gift *Gotte* has given her. I saw that when she effectively calmed Jacob. It's like her sole purpose is to work with difficult children."

Noah flinched at the word *difficult* and waited for Elam to state what the elders and Bishop Mueller's wife had about sparing the rod. Jacob wasn't spoiled. According to the specialist they'd seen, Jacob didn't know how to regulate his emotions, and Lydia seemed to think a lot of that was because he didn't communicate. No, that's not what she'd said. Jacob did communicate, it was the people around him who didn't understand what he was saying. Was she right?

"I'm not saying she has all the answers for you and Jacob, but I believe if you give her a chance, you won't regret it."

Oh, he was already regretting it, but he wouldn't say that aloud. The reasons for his regrets ranged from his privacy being invaded to being kept awake all night with revolving thoughts alternating between Lydia and his late wife. He'd married Collette and he didn't want to dishonor their marriage by thinking about another woman, especially one who'd been his first choice. Not that he hadn't loved his late wife—he had. But if Lydia had shown any interest in him as more than a friend, and Collette hadn't been in trouble, he never would have married Collette. "I'm giving her a chance. Two weeks."

Noah didn't think he could hold out against Lydia's infectious charm any longer than that, and he'd have to make sure he vacated the house whenever she was around. Elam was smart, having at least one of her sisters chaperone her. Not that he worried anything would happen between them, but still, caution was good.

Elam folded his arms and rested them on the handle of the shovel. "And if Jacob shows improvement?"

Noah walked the perimeter of the pad to see if it was a level area. "I haven't thought that far," he said. "I'm not saying she isn't good at her job, I just know my son."

Elam nodded, keeping silent, and Noah thought that took more wisdom than to speak whatever was obviously on his mind. They spent the next hour laying formwork for the base of the two chicken coops, mixing cement and then pouring it. Noah stood back and watched Lydia's *bruders* work under Elam's instructions. Silas, seventeen, helped eleven-year-old Remmy with the screeding. They drew a two-by-four over the top of the wet cement to make it level while Elam went behind them with a trowel. Isaiah, fifteen, worked with nine-year-old Pauly as Noah troweled behind them on the second coop, carefully following Elam's instructions.

Without waiting for Elam's okay, the boys began gathering the tools to take them to the pump to clean. Elam, tall and lanky with a full graying beard, smiled. "Looks *gut, jah*?"

"They do," Noah said. "I'm impressed with your *sohns*' work."

"Nothing better than accomplishing a good day's work with your *kinner*," Elam said, with a wink. "Silas started working with me about Jacob's age. Soon, you and Jacob will be working beside each other."

The sense of accomplishment he'd felt at seeing the cement pads completed suddenly washed away as if a torrential rainstorm had demolished their work. Jacob couldn't dress himself. He struggled with simple tasks like brushing his teeth and combing his hair. How would he ever be able to help pour cement?

The screen door slammed, the sound ricocheting across the yard like a crack of thunder, startling Noah from his thoughts. Bridget ran down the steps, Jacob chasing after her as Lydia appeared on the porch. She leaned against the railing, laughing. "Get her, Jacob, get her."

Bridget darted one way and then the next, encouraging Jacob to catch her. Noah's jaw fell slack at seeing his *sohn* actively play. Usually, he sat in his safe corner stacking blocks. Had he done his *sohn* a disservice keeping him isolated from other children?

Bridget slowed enough for Jacob to almost touch her and then jumped back. Jacob darted at her and touched her.

"Oh, no!" Bridget's voice trickled across the yard. "I'm it! You better run, Jacob."

"Run, Jacob," Lydia called out, adding to the game as she hiked her skirt and ran down the steps toward Jacob. She took his hand and led him away from Bridget, just as Bridget jumped at them.

Jacob threw his head back and giggled, the sound warming Noah's heart much like the day he'd held him for the first time after he was born. Lydia and Jacob ran around the wheelbarrow. "Me, me, me."

"You can't catch me," Lydia sang with him, taunting Bridget to chase.

"You should join them," Elam said. "There's nothing left to do here until tomorrow."

"*Denki!*" Noah didn't waste any time and strode to the place where the *kinner* and Lydia played. "Let's get him," he told Bridget once he was close enough.

He kept his pace slow, giving Jacob and Lydia enough space to keep out of their reach. His child's laughter filled him with so much joy that he stumbled over his feet and tumbled to the ground. He rolled to his back and found three sets of eyes looking at him. Jacob threw his little body on top of his and cupped Noah's face between his chubby hands. Worry clouded his eyes.

"I'm okay, Jacob," he said, "but I'm going to get you."

Just as Noah was about to wrap his arms around his son, Jacob jumped to his feet and hid behind Lydia.

"Uh-oh," Noah said, pretending to look around. "Where'd Jacob go?"

Bridget caught on. "Oh, Jacob, where are you?"

Jacob peeked from behind Lydia. "Me. Me."

"Let's get him," he said, winking at Bridget and rolling to his feet.

Lydia laughed. She backed away, all while keeping hold of Jacob so he wouldn't fall. She swung Jacob onto her hip. He wrapped his legs and arms around her waist and neck, clinging.

"Mmm, mmm," Jacob muttered as he pointed in a clear direction. Lydia darted around a tree, putting the large maple between them and Bridget.

"Where should we go next, Jacob?" Lydia asked and then obeyed the direction of his son's pointed finger. It wasn't long before Elam and Lydia's brothers joined in the game of tag, and soon they were all sitting on a quilt under a shade tree drinking lemonade and eating sandwiches.

The constant furrowed brow marring his *sohn*'s features was gone as he nibbled his sandwich. His child looked content. More than that, he looked at peace.

For the first time since Collette's death, Noah felt

grief's talons release their hold on him. He glanced across the blanket at the woman granting him permission to live outside the boundaries he had imposed on himself and his son, then at her siblings, who seemed to accept Jacob and didn't shy away from him.

Remmy, one of Lydia's younger brothers, jumped to his feet. "Can I take Jacob to see the goats?"

Noah looked at Lydia for her opinion.

She shrugged. "That is up to his *daed*."

Elam stood off the blanket. "If you don't mind, I'll take them."

"Of course," Noah said. "I believe I promised a young lady I'd teach her to milk a goat. I'll be down after I help Lydia clean up."

Elam dipped his head. "Come along."

Remmy and Pauly grasped Jacob's hands and took the lead. Elam and Silas walked side by side. Isaiah tugged on one of Bridget's *kapp* strings. She swatted his arm, and Noah laughed at the sibling affection he witnessed. When he'd thought of courting Lydia several years ago, he imagined a life like this. When he'd married Collette, that image had faded into something different. After her death, it had disappeared altogether, leaving him and Jacob in a lonely, isolated world. Now, he was beginning to feel that dream stir. And that was dangerous to his state of mind, and worse, his heart.

He glanced back at the woman who'd given him so much today as she worked on packing their makeshift picnic. He'd have to take the moments he'd granted her for the next two weeks and bottle them up in his memories. Once her time was over, he'd send her on her way and be grateful for what she'd given them. He couldn't risk allowing her more time to weasel her sunlight into his dark world.

"*Denki*," he said.

She lifted her face to him, her green eyes glittering with emotion. "It was fun, *jah*?"

"*Jah*, it was."

Later that night as he lay in bed staring up at the ceiling, he wondered how he'd keep from being swallowed up by Lydia Beachy, especially when he craved more moments like they'd had today.

Chapter Six

Lydia pulled the buggy in front of Samantha's Collective and set the brake.

"Let's go, Lydia," Alice said. "I want to see the *bopplin*."

"We're here to quilt, not play," Jessie said, sounding too much like their *mamm*.

Lydia released the latch on the door and climbed out to let her sisters scramble down. "There will be time to play, but remember to ask April first."

Alice and Bridget raced inside before she finished her sentence.

Crossing her arms, Jessie pursed her mouth. "Will they ever quit acting like children?"

Laughing, Lydia wrapped her arm around her younger sister and gave her a side hug. "If I recall, Jessie, it wasn't that long ago you raced from the buggy to choose flowers at Butterfly Gardens."

Jessie shrugged off Lydia's hug. "That was different. I was excited to see what was new."

"And your sisters can't be excited about something?"

"Like you get excited whenever you go to Noah's," Jessie taunted, and then laughed.

"I don't get excited," she said. *Nervous,* jah, *but not excited.*

"Sure, you do. You get all doe-eyed while packing your bag of goodies for Jacob."

"I do not," Lydia said, and if she did it was only because she imagined the successes with Jacob. Of course, she couldn't help imagining Noah's smile too at seeing his *sohn*'s progress, but that was beside the point. Especially since Noah had made himself scarce the last two days, ever since their game of tag. She couldn't help wondering if she'd done something wrong. She had to keep reminding herself she wasn't there for Noah, anyway.

"Noah and Lydia kissing in a tree," Jessie sang, and then darted away when Lydia reached for her. Her sister gripped the knob to Samantha's Collective and turned toward her. "Mark my words, my *schwester*. It won't be long before you're courting Jacob's *daed*."

Jessie disappeared into the store, leaving Lydia to contemplate her words. Was she trying to gain Noah's attention through his son? No, that wasn't her intention. She was only keeping a promise. But she couldn't help the thought intruding. If Noah turned his attention toward her, would it be such a bad thing? Could she do that to Collette without feeling guilty about living the life her friend should have? Would she be okay being his second choice?

Shaking off the thoughts, she stepped inside the store. Several folding tables were placed in the center of the large room. Quilt blocks were stacked on one table while various fabrics were on another.

April Stoltzfus looked up from her task of depositing scissors on one of the tables. "Hello," April said. "It is *gut* to see you, friend."

Lydia closed the distance between them and hugged her friend. "It is good to see you, too, April. How are the *kinner* and Esther?"

April motioned to the alcove in the corner where Lydia's *schwestern* played with the *bopplin.* "As you can see, the *kinner* are doing well. Esther is in Malachi's office making tea."

Her friend, April, once a widow, had married Malachi Stoltzfus in the fall, and birthed the child of her late husband shortly after. Malachi had been caring for his infant nephew and great-aunt when April came to Garnett.

"I can't wait to see Esther. It's been a while," Lydia said. Esther wasn't her aunt by blood, but she'd been like an aunt to her and her siblings for as long as she could remember.

"I can say by her enthusiastic chatter, she is excited to see you, too." April leaned closer and whispered, "I'd say she's excited to see everyone today, but she's only been asking after you."

Lydia clenched her teeth. She hoped Esther didn't know she'd been visiting Noah and Jacob each day. "That is curious, April. I wonder why. Surely she's just as eager to see Naomi and my *mamm.*"

Eyebrows raised, as if surprised by Lydia's response, April shrugged. "I can't say, but I'm sure we'll all discover the source of her excitement soon enough."

That's what Lydia was afraid of.

"Anyhow, Jeb is trying to walk, and Daisy is crawling. Esther has her moments where she forgets who the *kinner* are, but she keeps us on our toes," April said. "And how are you enjoying the summer now that school is out?"

"Fine. I am working with Noah Beiler's *sohn*," Lydia said and quickly wished she hadn't.

"My late husband's cousin? I have heard a lot about him from Esther," April said, once again giving Lydia a look as if she knew more than she was willing to admit. "But I have yet to meet him. Esther tells me he is a single *daed* after losing his wife to cancer." April pulled another pile of fabric from a cardboard box and placed it on the table. "I have been meaning to pay a visit, but with two infants and the store I don't have much time to get away. How is his *sohn*? Esther tells me Noah hasn't been to church in some time due to his son being trying at times. Oh, I am sorry. I shouldn't talk about others, even family, but Esther worries over all her great-nieces and nephews and I'm privy to her anxious conversations."

That's what Lydia was afraid of. It wasn't their way to speak about others, but there was some concession among family members, and a lot of grace where their elders were concerned when they did say things better left unsaid, especially when it bordered on gossip.

"It's fine, April. I imagine now that Malachi is happily married with a *wunderbar fraa*, her focus has shifted to Noah, Levi and Jared."

"Oh, *jah*," April said, giggling. "As well as the rest. She has been talking about visiting Haven, Kansas to see her great-nieces Emma, Sadie and Clara. She said they are growing too old to remain unmarried and childless."

Lydia held her gasp in check. She had met the sisters a few years ago when they came to Abe and Naomi's wedding. They weren't much different in age than Lydia. In fact, Clara was only a year younger than Lydia. Did that mean she was growing too old, too? Had she missed her chance at having a family of her own? Sure, she'd considered her age and had been annoyed with Gideon for pointing out she was growing older, but she'd never considered the truth of it. Not until now.

Had she spent too much time running from a schoolgirl's heartache by working with children at the school? If only things had been different. If only she'd told Noah how she felt before he had started courting Collette, but she hadn't. Instead, she'd sat by and watched love blossom between her two best friends in a very few short weeks, a love she could only hope for, all while keeping the truth locked inside her heart.

"Once again, I am speaking out of turn about things I have no business talking about. Are your *mamm* and Delphine coming today? Naomi, her *schwestern* and Abe's *mamm* said they'd be here, as well as Bishop Mueller's wife. Emmaline couldn't get away from Butterfly Gardens, this being their busy time of the year, but I assured her there would be many more quilt-ins to participate in."

"My *daed* and *bruders* are helping Noah rebuild his chicken coops and restore his flock. *Mamm* will be by after she takes them lunch. Unfortunately, Delphine is fighting a summer cold."

At least that's what Delphine had said before they left. However, she had seen the fear and anxiousness in her sister's eyes and the way she fidgeted with her hands. Delphine was happy and full of joy most days, not allowing her paralysis to affect her, but Lydia could only imagine being around Jared's family was unsettling. They'd rarely spoken about the accident, and even though her sister had forgiven Jared, being among friends and family where his name could so easily be mentioned had to make her sister nervous.

"Malachi told me about the illness plaguing Noah's chickens."

"Yes. It wiped out every bird. He's been grateful for the help. Before everyone arrives, I hoped to buy two pies and three different flavors of your jam." During her time with Jacob, she'd discovered he enjoyed jam and hoped to use the different ones to help teach him to communicate.

April pointed to a floor-to-ceiling shelf made of dark walnut. "Any flavors you have in mind? Esther and I made these yesterday."

"Blueberry, apricot and something vastly different, if you have them."

April's brow furrowed and Lydia laughed. She explained her intent behind the jams.

"That is genius, Lydia, and I'm sure you will meet with success. How about strawberry?"

The door swung open, and Hannah Lambright walked through.

"Hannah!" Jessie squealed, jumped to her feet and raced across the room before engulfing her friend in a hug. With their arms and heads bent together, the pair walked out the back door. Lydia looked out the bay windows to make sure they didn't leave the garden.

The rest of the Lambright *schwestern* trickled in, with Naomi Dienner and Abe's *mamm* following.

"What fun," Naomi said. "I'm so glad you thought of this, April."

"*Jah*," Rachel, one of Naomi's younger sisters, said. "It's a great way to bring our community together, and without the men to hover."

They all laughed.

"We have nothing if we don't have community," April said.

Esther hobbled in through the double doors with a loaded tray. Lydia raced over to relieve her of the load. "It's good to see you."

"How is my nephew doing?" Esther asked.

"*Gut*," she said, knowing she didn't fully speak the truth about Noah, whose heart had yet to mend. She glanced around the room to each woman and child present. These women were more than a community. They were family. But it wasn't her place to speak about how Noah was doing.

Noah's *mamm*, his sisters and sisters-in-law poured in with the sunlight. The room grew small, but it filled with so much love and joy at seeing each other. Her thoughts raced to the man who seemed lost and alone—the man she was determined to help reenter the community once again. She wondered if Noah had even pulled away from his own family because of Jacob's tantrums. When Talia, Noah's younger sister, made eye contact with her, Lydia feared she knew the answer.

Talia made a beeline across the room, weaving between the women of their community while nodding to each that she passed. Talia threw herself against Lydia, nearly knocking her over and embraced her in a hug. "*Denki*."

Lydia pulled back and searched the younger woman's eyes. She'd been a constant at their home before Delphine's accident. Delphine and Talia had been closer and inseparable, but Lydia still considered Talia her dear friend, too. The hope she saw in her eyes now sent her stomach roiling. "For?"

"For what you're doing with Noah and Jacob."

She released Talia, but didn't move too far away. "You know?"

"I think everyone knows, and we couldn't be happier." Talia leaned in and lowered her voice to a whisper. "We haven't seen him, since the Sunday before last, but just knowing you're there supporting Noah and Jacob has removed the tightness of *mamm*'s brow, and I've caught her singing, Lydia. Singing!"

"Shhh," Lydia said, reminding Talia that they were among many ears.

"Sorry, it's just *wunderbar*."

The roiling in Lydia's stomach pushed into her throat. "Excuse me, I need a drink of water."

Lydia walked over to the watercooler and grabbed a paper cup from the holder. She filled it with water and gulped it down, hoping to settle her stomach.

"Better?"

Lydia squealed and glanced around the room, taking note of each woman eyeing her and Noah's sister as if they were keeping secrets.

Talia giggled. "I didn't mean to startle you, but I'm so excited I can barely contain it."

Shaking her head, Lydia asked, "Why?"

"Because you're an answer to my prayers for my stubborn *bruder*. I knew if anyone could bring him to see reason it would be you, and *Gotte* is seeing it through."

"Talia, I don't think—"

"We've all heard about the work you've done at the

school, with some of the children who are…are like Jacob. You have given us hope."

"I really don't think—"

"You're giving Noah back to us, and granting us access to my nephew, too."

"Talia," Lydia bit out, and was satisfied at the look of concern in her friend's eyes. "You must know each child is different, as is each parent and their willingness to *listen* to their child. What I'm doing doesn't have guaranteed results." She knew this all too well. "And even if my working with Jacob has some success, I can say for certain there will still be hard days."

Even as Lydia said the words, she heard the doubt, and she regretted it. How could she convince Noah to believe in what she was doing with Jacob, and in Jacob himself, if she had doubts, too? But she didn't want Noah's family to pin all their hopes on her, especially since a great deal of Jacob's growth depended on Noah's involvement, and given his absence the last few days, that equated to nothing.

"Is that all?" Talia said, laughing. "I thought you were going to tell me Noah pushed you away."

He had, but not from Jacob, which was something. "No, I don't want your hopes to grow when there is a high probability what I'm doing won't work."

Lydia needed more time than Noah had given them. She wanted to tell her friend Noah needed long-term help with Jacob, help only an understanding and caring *fraa* could offer. Jacob needed full-time support, support in ways only a loving *mudder* could give with the right tools. And even then, days would be difficult. The task with Jacob would take a supportive, loving and grace-filled community, but they needed education on ways to help Noah and Jacob when they needed it, not judgment and ridicule. And Noah needed to give the community another chance.

"Where's your faith, Lydia?" Talia asked, and when Lydia just stared at her without responding, she said, "No big deal. I have enough faith for all of Garnett, because I know *Gotte* is bigger than your doubts and my *bruder*'s, my friend."

Lydia watched Talia stroll away and hug April before making her way to the *bopplin* and Lydia's sisters in the alcove. The younger woman wore peace like a second skin, as if she really believed all she'd just said. Lydia inhaled and released her breath on a shudder as she silently prayed she wouldn't fail, because everyone needed their family and community. Everyone needed connection, even the single *daed* of what their community and his family considered a troubled child.

A twinge of excitement swirled in Noah's stomach at the sound of crunching wheels coming up the drive. The excitement was quickly replaced with disappointment when he recalled Lydia wouldn't be coming today due to his own rules. No weekends.

Jacob didn't understand weekends and trying to explain to his *sohn* that Lydia wasn't coming to see them was nearly impossible. Not nearly—it was impossible. For him at least. Lydia would have had it handled in no time. But then Lydia was the current issue at hand.

"D-d-d?" Jacob cried as he pointed to the buggy through the screen door. In the last three hours, and through a lot of fumbling around on his part, he'd come to learn *D* was Jacob's word for Lydia.

"No, Jacob. That's not Lydia. It's her *mamm*, Malinda."

Noah spoke to him as if his *sohn* understood. Watching Lydia with Jacob for the last several days had influenced his behavior and how he communicated with his son, but the outcome was the same. At least for him. Of course, he'd kept his distance and often only watched her actions. It might have served them both better if he'd actually been close enough to hear their conversations, but after their game of tag the other day, when he'd felt more joy than he'd felt in a long time, all he wanted to do was hide. He feared if he accepted more moments like that with Lydia and Jacob, that it would all disappear.

Jacob screamed, dropped to the floor faster than an egg rolling off the counter, and began kicking his feet. Any other day, or any other day before Lydia, he would have picked his son up and carried him to the safe corner and held him until he calmed. But this wasn't any other day. Jacob's tantrums had escalated beyond the number of fingers Noah had on his hands, and he was exhausted.

Exhausted and frustrated. The fact Lydia's *daed* and *bruders* had been out back hammering away on the chicken coops, work they couldn't do the last two days when Lydia had been here because of the unexpected rain only frustrated him more.

Lydia's *mamm* climbed down from the buggy and pulled a picnic basket from the seat. Noah left his son on the floor where he flailed around kicking and squealing in the kitchen, and rushed down the stairs to help her carry the basket.

"Here, let me, Malinda," he said as he held his hand out for the basket.

"*Denki*, Noah," she said. "How is everything going?"

"Are you asking after Elam and your *sohns*?" He paused and bent his ear toward the tantrum slicing through his ears. "Or asking after Jacob?" He tried to laugh, but it came out half-hearted.

Lydia's mother touched his forearm with her hand as she searched his eyes. "I'm asking after you, Noah."

Something inside of him cracked a little, and he cringed as the mask he'd carefully kept in place for so long disintegrated in the face of kindness. And he blamed Lydia, this woman's daughter, and yet somehow his irritation for making him weak was overcome by his longing for Lydia's presence.

He'd kept his distance from her after the game of tag. And for good reasons. That day had been *wunderbar* beyond his imaginings. It had given him joy and hope. It almost renewed his faith that *Gotte* hadn't abandoned him completely. It had also left him with a desire he had no right to long for: something more than waking in the morning to battle with his son, only to be followed by a sleepless night while he considered his life alone, in a tomb of isolation.

The elder version of Lydia asking after his well-being only made him want everything Lydia had to offer even more. Friendship, companionship, laughter and her family. Not that his family was bad, but moments with them were always uncomfortable and awkward at best, even before Jacob's birth. "I am *gut*—"

Malinda Beachy raised a brow, as he'd seen her do

whenever one of her children tried to pull something over on her.

Noah shook his head. "No, I'm not *gut*. My *sohn* is not *gut*. Jacob misses Lydia."

He missed Lydia, too. And he could kick himself for not hanging around to watch her calm Jacob during his tantrums, or rather, watch her redirect him before a tantrum occurred.

He missed the peace he felt in her company, as if everything was right as rain, as his elderly *Englischer* neighbor often said.

"That is *gut*, *jah*?" Malinda turned toward the house.

Yes and no, but since he couldn't answer one way or the other, he shrugged.

"I see," Malinda said and halted their progress. "Have you ever heard the proverb 'Hard work makes the bread sweeter, faith makes the burden lighter'?"

"*Mamm* used to recite that proverb every time she pulled out the washboard."

Malinda laughed and then resumed walking. "Laundering little boys' clothes will force that proverb right out of a *mudder*, that's for certain."

"Boys' clothes," he said as he followed her up the steps. "As I recall, Lydia, Delphine and my *schwester* Talia spent more time in the mud than my *bruders* and I."

Lydia's *mamm* laughed harder. "They did, didn't they?" She pulled open the screen door, promptly sat beside Jacob, and then looked up at Noah. "I can't say Lydia and Delphine have changed much in that aspect, but at least they help with the washing now."

"I suppose that's something, *jah*?"

"Hello, Jacob. Do you mind if I sit with you?" she

asked as she patted her lap. His son quieted as if someone had hit the power switch, and he climbed onto Malinda's lap. She wrapped her arms around him when he laid his head against her shoulder. "Lydia can be a gale storm when she puts her mind to something, but she means well, Noah."

Noah sat the basket on the kitchen table then leaned against the countertop. "Always has been, *jah*?"

That's why he thought he had liked her when he was a youth. Why they'd been good friends. She had never shied away from any of the competitive ideas he and his friends came up with, and often went above and beyond their expectations, even at the cost of breaking her arm.

Malinda nodded. "That's right. I suppose by now you're regretting bowing to Lydia's persuasion to help your *sohn*, but the bread will be that much sweeter when she succeeds."

He was taken back by the confidence Malinda had in Lydia's capabilities. "You have that much faith in your daughter?"

A brilliant smile spread across Malinda's face. "I do, as all parents should in their children whenever they put their minds to *gut* things. And I have a lot of faith that *Gotte* has placed this task on her heart to complete for a reason." She looked down at Jacob and took his small chubby hand in hers, the loving gesture like that of a *grossmammi* with her grandchild. His own *mamm* had distanced herself from Jacob when he became too much to handle, and Noah had to fight the jealousy that his *sohn* was being robbed of what should be a given for any child, even one like his.

He pulled his attention from the tumultuous thoughts

wreaking havoc on his mind and his heart. He didn't resent his *mamm* for her choices, or any of his family. They still saw each other often, and he still went for Sunday dinners with Jacob, but it wasn't the same. They were wary of Jacob, and he supposed for good reason. At least they tolerated him and Jacob for a short time during family dinners, but he always kept Jacob close, especially after he'd overheard his *mamm* whisper to one of his sisters-in-law that Jacob was too much. The comment had hurt more than Noah expected. His *daed* made his displeasure known when Noah intervened before his father could take a switch to his *sohn*'s bottom. That was a moment Noah didn't relish reliving.

"That's not the point I'm trying to make," Malinda said, as she looked past his shoulder.

He wasn't trying to be obtuse, but the morning had been difficult to say the least, and he just couldn't see or think beyond the hopelessness he currently felt. A hopelessness he knew would dissipate, eventually, but at the moment, he felt like he was being swallowed by despair. "I'm sorry, Malinda. I'm not certain what sweet bread and washing clothes has to do with Lydia working with my son."

Her smile was borderline pity. Another reason he'd kept himself from the community. He didn't need or want pity. He wanted acceptance for his *sohn* without the cruel guidance of using the rod freely whenever Jacob acted out.

"What do you see when you set out to plow the fields?"

It'd been two years since he'd been able to work the fields because the days were long—not for him, but for whoever he'd left Jacob with while he completed the work.

His younger sister, Talia, had offered to watch Jacob, but given his father's belief Jacob needed punishment, he'd declined politely and allowed his fields to lie fallow. He closed his eyes and tried to recall the moment he'd climbed onto the seat and signaled for the horses to walk the fields. The warmth of the sun cloaking his shoulders, the sound of the harnesses jingling as the draft horses navigated the length of the field, the pull of the plow behind him as it churned up the previous season's hardened remains. The smell of Earth welcoming the cultivating alarm after its long winters' slumber.

He felt his mouth curve upward and warmth bathe his cheeks as he imagined the scent of freshly tilled dirt and the reins in his hands, knowing the week's work was the beginning of what would yield a crop to help feed his family and neighbors. The capability of his hands working with *Gotte* to give life to the fields, and fill bellies. He opened his eyes, realizing what Malinda was trying to teach him. "I see remnants of last season's crop entwined with weeds and large clumps of hard earth."

"Yes, and how do you feel when you first set the plow?"

He felt himself standing a little higher and his shoulders set squarer. "Determined—and satisfied."

Lydia's *mamm* nodded. "Why satisfied when the hard work has only begun?"

Noah moistened his lips, and then took in a hesitant breath, knowing this woman who'd been as much like his *mamm* as his own was trying to give him a bit of wisdom he wasn't sure he was ready to receive, but he couldn't leave her question unanswered. And he couldn't lie, either. "Because I know what the fruits of my labor will bear."

"And when you come across a particularly hard patch

of ground, or a piece that has never been plowed?" she asked quietly as Jacob's eyes began to fall shut.

"It can be difficult and take several more passes. Sometimes, I have to rest the horses and hack away at it with a pickax."

"So, it is harder for a moment until the rough patches are worked out?"

"*Jah*," he said.

She smiled, a knowing look as if she was making her point and he was missing it all together. "Do you carry the burden of fear that storms will rip the fruits from the ground or drought will wither them to dust?"

"No, that worry doesn't belong to the plow," he said with hesitation.

"You are a wise man, Noah," she said. "The faith a farmer has that his hard work will yield *gut* and plentiful fruits makes the burden of his work light because he *knows* what will happen when he completes the work, and the fruits of his labor are that much sweeter, *jah*?"

"What Lydia is doing is different," he said, fully believing it as truth. "She is working with the impossible. Plowing fields is something that has been done since the beginning of time with proven results." He flung his hand out in front of him as if to encompass his home and his child. "This is different. I haven't been here before."

"No, you haven't, but Lydia has. All you have to do is have faith that her work will yield *gut* fruit."

Chapter Seven

The chatter dissipated to a low murmur as Lydia's focus turned to laying several quilt blocks out on the table. It was often this way when she became engrossed in a project, tuning out the rest of the world so she could concentrate on a singular task. It was both a blessing and a curse as she'd often forgotten about cookies in the oven or pasta boiling in a pot.

She flipped a fabric piece upside down, and then another. Standing back, she examined the effect and sighed. She changed some more pieces but wasn't quite satisfied with the placements. However, she was growing bored with the tedious task and was itching to see the individual finished squares become one, even if there was no rhyme or reason to the pattern.

Lydia leaned over the mock design and turned all the pieces until all the dark brown ones formed a square. She rested her chin on her knuckles and laughed at the irony. "Well, if I was going to do that, I should have left them in squares instead of cutting them into triangles."

She stacked the fabric pieces together, sat in the folding chair, and rested her elbows on the table with her hands cradling her cheeks. Jessie giggled from somewhere behind her and she was fairly certain her sister was huddled in the corner with Hannah. They'd helped her cut several squares into triangles but quickly lost interest in the task, leaving Lydia by herself. She supposed the topic of their latest crush, Samuel Mueller, was more interesting than helping her make a quilt with "dull" colors, as Jessie called them.

Lydia refocused on the five-by-five squares made with two triangles, one side a soft color, the other chocolate. Simple. But the combinations fell far short of what she had hoped would create a striking effect.

She'd chosen the light colors in pale shades of greens, blues and tans without too much thought, but when she'd cut them into triangles, she'd known that wasn't true—she'd picked them because the colors were known to be calming and perfect for Jacob. The shapes were mirror images of the magnetic tiles he liked. She wasn't sure why he was particular to the triangles, often sifting through the pile of tiles until he'd isolated them from the squares. The squares remained in the bag, and even when she had tried to introduce one into his activity, he'd vehemently shaken his head until she returned it to the bag. She wondered if Noah had noticed such things. Was that why he always cut Jacob's peanut butter and jelly sandwiches into triangles?

She returned her attention to the quilt. If she was going to give this quilt to Jacob, she'd have to finish it within the week. Unless *Gotte* answered her prayers and granted her more time.

"Guess that means I can't quit yet," she said as she picked at the corners of the stack, thumbing through the pieces. She pulled the top two off and laid them back out, then the next two. Jessie had been right: The colors were dull. No matter how she arranged them in an attempt to accentuate each of the muted colors sewn to solid dark brown, nothing seemed to work.

A gnarled hand appeared on the fabric, pulling Lydia's attention from her thoughts. She looked up and saw Esther drawing her finger along the sewn lines.

"An interesting choice of colors," Esther said.

"*Denki*," she said. "I've been told they're boring."

"Youth—so eager to teach when they've yet to live wisdom," Esther said as she took three blocks from the stack and laid them beside the two Lydia had been toying with.

Lydia glanced over her shoulder at her sister as she mentally unpacked Esther's words and found a lot of truth in them. Jessie often held strong opinions on matters but rarely had the lived experience to understand whether what she said was true or not.

"But it works. Dark and light, opposing forces. Makes me wonder who you intend the quilt for."

Lydia knew her smile was weak. "No one in particular."

"Mmm," Esther mumbled. She flipped each piece, so the brown was on the bottom while alternating tan, blue, green.

Tilting her head, Lydia contemplated the pattern, and then repeated it until there were nine across. Esther started the second row, this time beginning with blue, green and then tan. They placed several more rows, and Lydia was pleased with the ombré appearance. "I like it," Lydia said, finally envisioning how the other rows would fall into place. "It'll be perfect."

"For?" Esther asked with a knowing, raised eyebrow.

Lydia shook her head. "No one in particular," she said, not wanting to admit even to herself she played the hopeful coming scene in her head of when she gifted Jacob with the blanket. Mostly she didn't want to admit she imagined Noah's pleased reaction at the gift.

"Speaking of no one in particular, how are my great-nephew Noah and my great-great-nephew Jacob doing?"

Lydia should have expected Esther's inquiry after her conversation with April, but her bluntness still surprised her. She shrugged. "Fine, I suppose."

"Mmm," Esther mumbled again as she looked straight into Lydia's eyes. "Something tells me you know more than you're saying. I believe you have a strong opinion on the matter of my nephews' well-being."

Lydia felt as if she was under a magnifying glass, the kind they used to follow ants around as kids. She had an opinion on the matter? What was that supposed to mean? Anyway, her opinion didn't matter if Noah didn't heed her guidance. "I've barely seen Noah, and my time with Jacob has only been a few hours. Hard to form an opinion about how someone is doing when so little time is spent with them."

Esther laughed. "I guess my curiosity got the best of me. I know Noah has a *mamm*, and I'd ask her about them, but you and your family have seen them more than anyone."

"Have you tried visiting them?" Lydia asked, trying to keep her tone soft and even, without the taint of irritation.

"Suppose I could, if nephew Malachi would allow me the use of the buggy. He's too busy to bother with an old woman, and April has her hands full," Esther said as she laid another triangle block down to form another row. "My mind isn't what it used to be."

Lydia's cheeks heated with shame. "I'm sorry, Esther. I spoke without thinking."

Esther cackled. "No need to apologize to me. I often speak without thinking. Just ask April. Now, how are my nephew Noah and his *fraa*, Collette, doing?"

The question startled Lydia, but she quickly schooled her features so Esther didn't suspect she had said something she shouldn't have. But how was she to answer? If she reminded Esther of the truth, would it cause her to grieve again? Would she grow more confused, or even become frustrated for forgetting something so important?

"Esther," April said, pulling out a chair from the table. "Why don't you sit a while."

"Yes, I think that would be good." Esther lowered herself onto the seat next to Lydia and then glanced at her. "Oh, Lydia. It's *gut* to see you. How are you doing?"

She breathed a sigh of relief that Esther had shifted her mind from Noah, even as her heart ached for Esther, April and Malachi. How did they manage day-to-day when they never knew what each moment would bring? When Lydia woke up, she knew the tasks ahead of her, and for the most part there was an unspoken schedule when it came to chores. Some daily. Some weekly. "*Gut.* I'm enjoying my summer so far."

Having talked enough with April over the last few months, and seeing the severity of Esther's mental decline, she wondered how April was able to pivot with Esther's needs, while effectively keeping her house in order and running a successful business. Her thoughts raced to Noah, and she decided to seek April's guidance on how her friend managed so well so she could offer Noah some more unsolicited advice.

"*Gut, gut.*" Esther picked a loose string dangling from one of the blocks, and Lydia cringed at having missed cutting it. "How is Noah? You've been such a *gut* friend taking care of Collette while she's been ill."

Lydia swallowed the knot forming in her throat. She didn't feel like a *gut* friend. It had taken her over four years to keep her promise to her late friend. She'd left Noah to care for his young son as he navigated life without his wife. "*Denki.*"

April touched her hand, and Lydia swiped away the tears forming at the corner of her eyes.

"You're a *gut* Amish woman, Lydia," Esther said. "Noah would be blessed to have you as his *fraa.*"

Lydia blinked. "Oh, no, Esther, we're not getting married."

"Aunt Esther likes to believe she is a matchmaker," April said. "She matched Malachi and me."

"It is a *gut* match, too," Esther said.

"I agree," April said.

Lydia was glad the topic had moved off her and Noah, but she couldn't help replaying the last four years in her mind. Why had she walked away from Noah? He had been one of her closest friends, along with Collette. Had she done so for selfish reasons? She'd tried to tell herself he needed time, but in truth, she'd needed space, and not to grieve her friend. She'd had plenty of time to grieve as Collette fought for her life and lost it. She'd been at her bedside during the worst and was able to rejoice, although with great sadness, that her friend no longer suffered.

The moment Collette took her last breath, Lydia

had left Noah to his family and Collette's. Because she feared she no longer held a place in his life, or in little Jacob's. And if she'd tried to continue their friendship as they'd been before his marriage to Collette, she feared what others might say—that she was trying to become Noah's new wife, which wouldn't have been too far from the truth since she'd felt so much pain on his behalf. All she wanted to do was hold Jacob for comfort, and to hold Noah until he no longer hurt.

No, she hadn't needed time; she'd been a coward and run from the hollowness she'd seen in Noah's eyes. More than that, the fear of what she might have discovered lying beneath the surface of her own heart that had been festering from the moment she'd discovered Noah and Collette were courting. Jealousy was an ugly thing, and she didn't want to admit she'd ever felt the emotion. But the truth was the jealousy that had lain beneath the surface for so long had reared its ugliness the moment Collette died, because it was as if the love he'd had for her had taken a large part of Noah, leaving him nothing more than a shell of himself, and now, she had to contend with the possibility that she may have wished Collette out of Noah's life. And that had angered her more than the unfairness of a husband and child losing the heart of their home. Once she kept her promise to Collette, she hoped to be free from the guilt plaguing her.

Noah eased the screen door open to keep the hinges from squeaking too loudly. Now that Jacob had fallen into an exhausted sleep, he didn't want to wake him, as he feared they would relive the entire day all over again, minus the moments Lydia's *mamm* had held him.

Noah sank into the rocker on the covered porch, leaned his head back and closed his eyes. The scratches on his arms from Jacob's little fingernails still stung, even with the coconut salve covering each minor wound. He sat forward and buried his head into his hands, thankful Jacob hadn't hurt Lydia's *mamm*, too.

"*Gotte*, what am I to do?"

Jacob didn't mean to cause harm to anyone. Noah believed that much. He wasn't sure what triggered Jacob's need to harm others when he was in the middle of a meltdown, and he certainly didn't know how to keep him from hurting others, like Lydia. But the scratches on his arms weren't at the front of his dilemma. It was whether he should allow Lydia to return on Monday or beg her to come tomorrow on the agreed day off.

If he allowed Lydia to return, he would only put off the inevitable when the next week was up. Five days of peace to be met with more days like today when Lydia didn't return. But if he told her the arrangement wasn't working, he'd break his word. She would be disappointed, and maybe even angry, but she would understand, especially if her *mamm* told her about Jacob's behavior. Still, he wasn't the sort of man to break his word.

He shoved his fingers through his hair and tugged a little, just to feel something other than this bone-deep exhaustion. Before his son had needed so much of his attention, he'd worked the fields from dawn to dusk, as well as tending to all the other chores. And yet he couldn't recall a day as exhausting as this one. Not even the days when he'd helped his *daed* tear down an old milking barn in the strong Kansas winds. And Malinda had even gave him a short reprieve today.

He didn't want to be released of Jacob. He loved his son deeply, but he was beginning to understand he needed help. Lydia's help, so it seemed. She was the only one besides her *mamm* who was unafraid of Jacob. *Even though they should be*, he thought while running his fingers over the gouges on his arm.

He stretched out his aching legs, and then folded them in. He felt restless. Hopeless, and yet something stirred within him as if there was an answer just within his grasp. He just couldn't see it yet.

Standing from the rocker, he stretched his arms, his back, and rolled his neck. The movements did little to release the tension that had been building all week—ever since Lydia and her family invaded his solitude.

"Have you no words of wisdom for me, *Gotte*?" Silence battered his ears, roaring like a swollen river racing to breech whatever walls it could. He waited a moment, hoping for a verse to enter his mind, or one of his *mamm*'s favored proverbs. Like the one Malinda quoted earlier. *Hard work makes the bread sweeter, faith makes the burden lighter.* Today had been hard, more than hard as his heart hurt each time Jacob fell into a tantrum. There was no sweetness at the end of the day, other than the soft, even breaths of his son's sleep.

The pink-and-purple twilight hugged the overgrown fallow fields, beckoning him to the freedom of work they offered. He meandered down the stairs and strode across the freshly cut yard. He'd have to remember to thank Remmy for mowing while the rest of them had worked on finishing up the chicken coops. Halting at the edge of the lawn, he tucked his thumbs into his suspenders and rocked back on his heels.

The first year he'd allowed the field to rest, it had been with the hope Jacob's difficulties were only for a season. And last year, his hope had dwindled until it disappeared, and he'd felt nothing but despair with no light for the future. Hope deferred had made his heart more than sick, not just for the crops he wouldn't grow, but for the child who'd never become mature in the ways of most children. But now Lydia tried to renew that hope that Jacob could do more, could be more than he ever imagined, and he was scared to believe it, scared that if Jacob didn't meet with Lydia's success, his heart would not just become sick, but shatter from disappointment.

He turned his focus from his thoughts, unwilling to think the worst and unable to hope for the best, and moved to the open field in front of him. It was too late in the season to plant corn or soybeans, but if he used the sickle bar mower, he could cut the field and prep it for winter wheat. He pushed his thumbs against his suspenders, stretching them taut, and then released them with the sting of the snap against his chest.

Jacob couldn't ride with him while he tended to the fields, and his *sohn* couldn't be left on his own while he did the work, not even for a few minutes or for the long hours it would take. He crouched and ran his hand through the tall grass and weeds.

His thoughts and heart were at odds. His son was imprisoned by an ailment and Noah feared it was because his heart hadn't been honest when he'd married Collette. He had yearned for a future with Lydia but refused to interfere with his friend Gideon's pursuit of her. He tore at the grass and tossed it. If only Gideon had never taken Lydia on a buggy ride, then maybe Noah wouldn't have married Collette, and Collette would be alive, and his son wouldn't have suffered from the difficult birth that left him developmentally delayed. Maybe, he'd be normal like other children, just slightly different as the autism would never go away as Lydia had taught him that over the last several days. She'd also shown him the *gut* qualities of Jacob's differences.

Noah rose and stared out across the field. An owl hooted from somewhere in the tree line and Noah thanked *Gotte* for the role the creature played in mice control. A tear rolled down his cheek. "Thank you for my *sohn*, *Gotte*." Even on difficult days, like today.

But could he willingly repeat a day like this tomorrow and cause Jacob undue stress, when all he needed to do was reach out to Lydia for help? And when Lydia's time was up with Jacob, could he let her offer of help go? No. His *sohn* had grown attached to Lydia in the short time she'd worked with him, as had Noah.

Was it fair to ask Lydia to sacrifice the rest of her summer to work with Jacob? Was it fair of him to expect results with his *sohn* when he didn't believe it was possible?

Lydia's *mamm* had spoken about the fields and how a farmer never doubted the yield of his crops when he planted seed. Experience was a *gut* teacher. He breathed in the evening air. It was true Lydia had experience with children like Jacob, but he feared the unknown. What if Jacob's tantrums were because of his inability to communicate? He shook his head, even as he laughed at himself. "No, according to Lydia, it's not Jacob's inability to communicate," he said to the field. But rather his own inability to listen and understand Jacob. Perhaps it was time he got over his stubbornness and allowed Lydia to teach him, too. Which meant spending more time with her. It would please her to know she'd won this battle, but she wouldn't gloat, not like she had when she'd beaten him and all his friends in a footrace in their youth. No, she would accept this one with grace. He paused, imagining Lydia's response when he approached her with his offer. She would accept the win with gratitude, because she believed in Jacob, and she wanted him to believe in his *sohn*, too.

"Well, then, Noah Beiler, even though it is Sunday tomorrow, how about you pay Lydia a visit and renegotiate her time?" That would make Jacob happy. Maybe he would arrive early enough to invite her to his family's Sunday dinner.

Chapter Eight

Lydia laid out the quilt blocks on the dining room table in the pattern Esther had helped her create. "What do you think?"

Delphine pushed her wheelchair around the table, inspecting the angles from each side. She glanced at Lydia with a raised brow. "You chose these colors?"

"*Jah*," she said, sounding offended even to her own ears. "What's wrong with them?"

Her *schwester* rolled closer to the table, and Lydia could tell her sister chewed on the inside of her cheek. "Not your typical pinks and purples when making your quilts for the market."

"No," Lydia said. "I wanted to try something different."

"For a boy?"

"What is wrong with that, Delphine?"

"Nothing, I suppose, except you're not admitting you're making this for Jacob. I wonder what Noah will think."

Lydia growled and began stacking the blocks one on top of another. "Never mind. I wanted to show you the pattern and how well it works, and all you can do is tease."

"I can't help wondering if your grumpiness has anything to do with not seeing Noah yesterday."

"That's it," Lydia said as she slammed the blocks in her hand down on the table. Lydia jabbed the latch on the screen door with her fingers.

"Where are you going?"

Lydia glanced over her shoulder and watched Delphine spin the wheelchair around. "For a walk! Maybe even to town. Before I say something, I might regret."

Lydia stalked down the stairs next to the ramp. The wheels of her sister's wheelchair clattered over the boards.

"You wouldn't," Delphine squealed. "It's five miles. *Mamm!*"

Bending toward her sister, she spoke through gritted teeth "*Mamm* isn't here. It's Sunday. She and *Daed* are out visiting, remember?"

"Walking to town is a little dramatic, don't you think, Lydia?"

"Not if it's getting away from you at the moment," Lydia snapped. "You're lucky I don't put frogs in your bed or loosen the lid on the flour."

"You're not a prankster, Lydia."

"No, I'm not, but I am tired of your teasing," she said, crossing her arms. "I am not interested in Noah."

She couldn't be.

Delphine snorted, and Lydia glared.

"Isn't it possible for me to make a blanket for a friend's child?"

Delphine's mouth flattened, and she said, "A friend who happens to be a single *daed* and in need of a wife?"

"I think he would argue the point." Lydia hadn't heard him talk about wanting to marry again, but she couldn't help but think about her conversation with Esther when she'd so bluntly stated what a *gut fraa* she'd make for

Noah. Of course, Esther had been in one of her mental slips, as April called it, but still, Lydia couldn't unhear the words and she couldn't stop daydreaming about the next time she saw Noah.

"See?" Delphine said. "Your shoulders slumped. Even you think he's in need of a wife."

Lydia pulled her shoulders back. "I didn't say that."

"No, you didn't have to say it with your words. Didn't you say communication is more nonverbal than verbal?"

Lydia rolled her eyes. "Doesn't mean I'm courting him through Jacob. I wouldn't do that. Besides…" She cut her words off before the rest of the thought raced out of her mouth.

"Besides what, Lydia?" Delphine asked. "If he wanted you for a wife he would have asked you instead of Collette?"

Lydia remained quiet. She disliked when Delphine read her thoughts so well.

"You forget I share a room with you. I am privy to your muffled tears." Delphine grabbed her wheels and turned her chair to face Lydia. "There is nothing wrong with following your heart."

Except she didn't want another broken heart, and how could she follow her heart? What if he did choose her this time? How could she live the life with Noah that she'd wanted as a young girl when her best friend couldn't? It wasn't fair that Collette had missed out on living life with Noah or experiencing her beautiful child with big emotions.

"It's complicated." Lydia sat on the bottom stair. Delphine descended the rest of the ramp and wheeled her chair to face Lydia.

"I don't see how. You like him, and you're *gut* with his *sohn*. All you need to do is convince him he needs you."

Lydia sighed, glanced at her sister and held her gaze, willing her to see the impossibility of her situation. "I don't want any potential *mann* to need me. I want them to love me, and I don't think Noah could do that." Especially if he knew about the guilt eating away at her.

"And you won't give him a chance to love you," Delphine said.

"No. I can't," she said. "Besides, I'd be his second choice. Just like Gideon's second choice."

"Second choice? What does that have to do with anything? So what, a widower can't find love again? I don't understand why you can't give him a chance, Lydia." Delphine leaned back against her wheelchair.

"Because I willed Collette's death," Lydia said as she squeezed her eyes closed against the tears pooling.

"What?" Delphine asked. "That is ridiculous."

Jumping to her feet, Lydia dusted her lavender dress. "I was jealous of her. She had everything I wanted. Everything I shared with her that I wanted. She knew as much as you did how much I liked Noah, but she courted him and married him, and she had never told me she'd liked him, too." And it all had happened so fast.

"Lydia, do you hear yourself?" Delphine reached out and took her hand. The comfort of her sister's touch shook her to the core, shattering her resolve not to cry. "You're not *Gotte*. Your will can't supersede His. You didn't cause Collette's cancer or her death."

"I know that in my head, but it's difficult to reconcile it in my heart." Lydia shrugged as she gave a half-hearted smile. "And the more I'm around Noah, the more guilt I feel. I know I shouldn't feel responsible for Collette's illness, but I do. And I could never accept a courtship with him without telling him the truth, and then I fear he'd never forgive me. I guess it's a *gut* thing I only have five days left with Jacob, huh?"

"You need to spend some time with *Gotte*, Lydia. You are withholding forgiveness from yourself, and you need to let it go. You also need to quit making excuses for *Gotte*. His will is His will. Did you ever think that maybe she would have gotten cancer no matter who she married?"

"When did you become so wise?" Lydia asked.

Delphine motioned toward her legs. "This. Losing the use of my legs to a foolish game will do that to a person. I could spend my days wishing I never would have gotten in that buggy with Jared, but I did."

"I'm sorry, Delphine," Lydia said, bending down to hug her sister. "Here I am whining, and I have no cause."

"Don't," Delphine said, and Lydia pulled back. "I didn't say that to get your sympathy or empathy but rather share with you that I understand. We all have regrets. What is that old proverb *Daed* used to quote whenever we wished for something different to have happened? 'Regrets over yesterday and the fear of tomorrow are twin thieves that rob us of the moment.'"

"*Jah*, like when you said you wished you wouldn't have eaten the entire tub of ice cream and would never eat ice cream again," Lydia teased, feeling much lighter than she had a few moments earlier.

"I was nine," Delphine countered.

"And none of us got ice cream, not even *Mamm* and *Daed*. I had to listen to you moan and groan all night."

"And hold the bucket for me."

"Hey, what are sisters for, right?"

"I'm returning that favor now, Lydia. Don't regret the jealousy you felt over Noah and Collette's relationship. Forgive yourself and move on. Just as you and I both know Collette would have forgiven you. Just as you had her when she married Noah. And don't let your fear of tomorrow's unknown rob you of what you deserve. Happiness. You've punished yourself long enough, don't you think?"

Had she? Is that why she shied away from any attention coming her way? Is that why she always said no to an Amish man who asked to take her for a buggy ride?

"Very well. I get your point, and to show I'm trying, the next time an Amish man asks me for a buggy ride, I won't say no."

Delphine laughed. "Even if it's Gideon?"

Lydia rolled her eyes and glanced up at the beautiful clear blue sky. Why hadn't she thought about that possibility? "Even if it's Gideon."

At that moment, buggy wheels crunched on the gravel. The sound raked over Lydia's nerves like two screeching cats. Gotte, *this is not funny*, she silently prayed and then peered down the drive. "What's Noah doing here?"

"Maybe he's come to ask you for a buggy ride," Delphine teased, and then wheeled her chair out of the way before Lydia could swat her.

"Unlikely. He's barely spoken to me since Tuesday." *Mamm* had told her about the trying time Noah and Jacob had yesterday, but when Lydia went to leave with the thought of rescuing the pair from each other, her *mamm* held her back, suggesting she give Noah time. "He's probably here to tell me not to bother coming back."

Delphine snorted. "Now that's unlikely. From what our *schwestern* say, he depends on you too much."

"Get your head out of the clouds, Del. Noah Beiler has done just fine on his own," she said, knowing the self-imposed isolation Noah had committed to was far from fine. At least not in her mind.

Noah parked the buggy near the house, stepped down and swung Jacob to his feet.

"D-d-d," Jacob screeched as he ran toward her. Jacob reached her and holding one arm up to be held, he tugged on her skirts with the other one.

"Please," she said as she signed to him.

"P—p—please," Jacob repeated. She smiled, her heart warming at his effort. Lydia glanced at Noah, wondering if he'd heard his *sohn*, but his eyes were shielded by his hat. She rubbed circles on Jacob's back as she watched Noah stride across the yard. Her pulse sped and her heart pounded in her throat. He'd been handsome in his youth, but handsome didn't come close to describing Noah now.

"Mark my words, Lydia," Delphine whispered. "He's here to ask you for a buggy ride, and if I'm right you can do my chores tomorrow."

"Hi, Delphine," Noah said before Lydia could respond to her sister.

"Noah, *gut* to see you," Delphine said as she turned her wheelchair toward the house, and then said in a firm voice, "Don't forget, you won't say no."

Noah watched Delphine use her arms to push her wheelchair across the yard with the efficiency of someone well used to their disability. He turned back to Lydia. "She's getting along well."

"She's a Beachy," Lydia said.

No longer able to avoid looking at her, he glanced down at her, crouching next to his son. The sun caught the light in her bright green eyes, making them appear the color of emerald stones he'd once seen at a farmers market. Her dark lashes brushed against her rosy cheeks as she blinked while speaking to Jacob in soft, hushed tones.

His mouth suddenly went dry and he wished for a glass of sun-soaked tea. "A rare trait, *for sure and for certain*."

Tilting her chin, she glanced up at him, lengthening the slender neck traveling out of her collar. The *kapp* strings swayed in the summer breeze. So much about Lydia Beachy spoke tender grace, but she hid it beneath a huge dose of stubbornness, especially when she fought for those she cared about. Like his son. And right now, he was grateful she had the strength and courage to challenge him. If she hadn't, Jacob would still be relegated to his safe corner without a thought as to what he might want or how to ask for it.

And as difficult as yesterday had been, Noah had to admit, his son had spoken his wishes. Maybe not in full sentences, not even in full words, but he'd made enough of a sound that Noah had had no doubts his son wanted Lydia. This beautiful woman's stubborn tenacity was bringing light to Jacob's world—as well as his, and he was certain it was the same stubborn tenacity her sister used to manage her paralysis.

Rising to her full height, Lydia turned Jacob and pointed toward the pigpen. When he'd first seen Lydia, Noah hadn't noticed the pigpen. Or the big barn, freshly coated in white paint, a reminder his needed a good scraping and fresh paint. He'd only seen Lydia and his son.

"See the piglets?" she asked. "Oink, oink."

Jacob's eyes grew wide, and then he doubled over and fell into a fit of giggles. The sound was infectious and a balm to Noah's soul, especially after the trials of yesterday. The sound of laughter coming from Jacob, intermingled with his deeper tones, wasn't completely unfamiliar to Noah, as he'd heard them the other day when they played their game of tag, but the feel of it, the giddiness of it shocked him all the same. And to think he'd nearly changed his mind about coming to see Lydia this morning, all because he was too scared of the unknown.

"Oink, oink," Lydia repeated, and then said, "Now your turn, Jacob."

"K-k," Jacob uttered.

"*Gut*, Jacob, very *gut*, *jah*?" she asked, her green gaze meeting his, encouraging him.

Noah needed a drink of tea. He paused while moistening his lips. He touched his hand to Jacob's shoulder. "*Jah*, very *gut*, Jacob."

His son jumped up and down, clapping his hands while making his pig sounds. Noah released Jacob's shoulder and reached for Lydia's hand. She snapped her attention to him, her eyes wide. There was so much he wanted to say to her as gratitude overwhelmed him, but all he could imagine was a simple, quiet *denki* before dropping his hand away from hers.

"Why are you here, Noah?"

Her bold question surprised him, and he couldn't help wondering if she was bothered by his appearance today. "I know it's Sunday, but Jacob and I discussed it." He paused at her raised eyebrow. "We, uh, wanted to invite you to *Mamm*'s for Sunday visiting and dinner."

Small wrinkles formed on her brow just below her *kapp*, her blond eyebrows pointing into a V.

"We don't go visiting, but we go to *Mamm* and *Daed*'s on the Sundays that we don't have church," he said.

Her chest rose, and he couldn't help noticing how she bit the inside of her cheek. "I see."

Her hesitation was akin to rejection, and he felt it as if he was hearing about her taking a ride with Gideon all those years ago. "If you have other plans, or would rather rest—"

"No," she said, shaking her head. "That's not it at all. It would be nice to visit with your family, although I did see Talia and your *mamm* yesterday. It's just, well, I haven't baked anything."

So, she wasn't rejecting him, not that he was asking her to court, only go visiting with him and Jacob. He allowed the tension in his shoulders to relax. "*Mamm* makes plenty," he said. "You know that. Besides, I'm sure everyone will be happy to see you." And maybe they'd be pleased enough that he wouldn't feel the sting of their disappointment when he and Jacob arrived. "What say you? Would you like to take a buggy ride with us?"

She flinched and looked past his shoulder toward her house. She blinked and then nodded. "Let me tell my sisters."

"Jacob, Jacob, please," she said, touching the *buwe*'s shoulder, and then waited for him to stop mimicking the pigs and look at her. "Would you like me to go on a buggy ride with you?"

Curious, Noah wondered why she asked Jacob's opinion, but when his son took both of their hands and they walked across the yard, the why didn't matter. For a moment, all seemed right in his world. Once they reached the bottom of the steps, she released Jacob's hand, told him she'd be right back, and then disappeared into the house. The separation, even though only a short time, renewed the loneliness he'd experienced over the last two years as Jacob's behaviors became more prevalent. The sensation left him at odds. He didn't like the isolation and loneliness, but he also didn't like the idea Lydia seemed to fill that void. He was growing to miss her during her absence, and he didn't like that, especially since his guilt over Collette's death was lessening the more time he spent with Lydia. They'd been blessed by Lydia's kindness as she took care of Collette and Jacob during her illness. He'd offered little help during those last months while he ran from the consequences of his reality and buried himself in the farm.

Delphine rushed through the screen door, her wheelchair banging against the doorframe as she grinned like a cat with her paws deep in cream. Lydia reached out to snag her sister, but Delphine was too quick. Lydia stopped in her tracks and brushed her palms down the front of her white apron. She lifted her chin and pulled her shoulders back as if to compose herself.

Delphine wagged her finger in Noah's direction. "I wouldn't be doing my duty as the second-eldest sister if I didn't tell you to have Lydia back before dark."

"Delphine," Lydia growled.

Noah missed being a part of this family when they had all been close. "Of course," he said, and then glanced at a red-faced Lydia. "Shall we?"

She nodded and then dipped back inside only to return

with a bag and a covered pie. Did he dare hope it was another shoofly pie for him?

"I thought you didn't make anything," he said.

She smiled. "I didn't. I purchased this yesterday at Samantha's Collective. Apple pie with a hint of jalapeno."

"Sounds interesting." He climbed the stairs and took the items from her, tucked them into the back of the buggy, and then assisted her onto the seat before helping Jacob to sit next to her.

Noah climbed in beside his son and released the brake as he exhaled the breath he didn't realize he'd been holding. He felt nervous, like it was his first time taking a girl on a ride. Which was silly, given he'd been married and had a *sohn.*

He stole a glance at Lydia, who had her eyes closed, her face lifted for the breeze's soft caress, her hands demurely settled in her lap. A soft smile teased the corners of her mouth as if she recalled a funny incident.

"What is it you're thinking, Lydia Beachy?"

Chapter Nine

His question intruded into the deepest part of her core, and she felt stripped bare and exposed as if he heard the mental dialogue racing through her head. Startled by the possibility, she flung her eyes wide-open and knotted her moist hands together.

He wanted to know what she was thinking, and she knew she couldn't tell him the truth. *Well, Noah, I was thinking about how I have waited for this moment since I was fourteen.* Only to have her dreams crushed when Noah had asked Collette to go on a buggy ride instead of her.

In her imagination, there hadn't been a lovely child sitting between them. She looked down at Jacob, his hat tilted upward revealing full rosy cheeks from the warm sun. His brilliant smile was genuine, authentic and bigger than life—as big as the bright blue sky above them, and just as encompassing. Having spent the last week with him, she knew he didn't do anything halfway, not even when it came to smiling.

"I really wasn't thinking about anything," she said. It wasn't a lie really because her thoughts were nothing. They couldn't be something. This was just a simple invitation to his family's Sunday dinner. Of course, she couldn't help wondering if the invitation was driven by the tantrums Jacob had yesterday.

"Really?" he asked. "Even with your eyes closed, you looked deep in thought. I think you had something on your mind."

"Just enjoying being out in the fresh air and feeling as if I'm one with the wind while riding in a buggy."

"Hmm," he mumbled.

"Hmm," she responded to his challenge, waiting for him to call her out in between Jacob repeating their sounds. "And the ride couldn't be better with such a handsome chaperone."

Noah snapped his gaze toward her, his eyes bright and his smile arrogant. Her cheeks burned hot, and before he could say anything, she rushed on to say, "I was talking about Jacob."

"Mmm-hmm," he mumbled, as he focused back on the dirt road.

"I was," she squeaked, and then moistened her lips. Before she could stop herself, she asked, "What if I wasn't?"

Noah kept his eyes trained ahead, but she noticed how his Adam's apple seemed to pause as if he was failing to swallow. Thankfully, he didn't say another word. She wasn't sure how she'd feel about his answer, no matter what it was.

"Look, Jacob, cows," she said, pointing at a group of cows grazing near the barbed wire fence on the other side of the ditch. The bright green grass painting the rolling hills spoke of *Gotte*'s creation, and it was just as good of a distraction as anything to move them out of the awkwardness she'd put them in. "Moo."

"Moo," Jacob repeated.

"*Gut.*" Lydia clapped. She smiled when Jacob clapped, too. "Moo. Oh, look, Jacob, donkeys. Hee-haw." Her voice cracked when the buggy wheel hit a rut in the road. "—caw."

Laughter rumbled within the cab of the buggy. Noah threw back his head and laughed. Jacob slapped his palm against his thigh and giggled.

"Eee-aaw, eee-aaw." Jacob sounded out the vowels in between his giggles.

"*Gut*, *sohn*, very *gut*," Noah said. "Much better than Lydia's."

"What?" she said, feigning offense. "What are you talking about? There is nothing wrong with my donkey sounds."

Noah broke into more laughter. "Not if your donkey is having a conversation with a crow."

"I did no such thing," she said as she sat back against the seat and crossed her arms. "It's not my fault you hit a rut."

"Eee-aaw, eee-aaw," Jacob said.

His little voice effectively reminded her she had an audience of more than just the man who was thoroughly irritating her. She needed to be careful to set a good example while she was upset and not let her anger at Noah's teasing get the best of her. She sat up, relaxed her arms and regained her composure. "That's right, Jacob."

"Are you sure it isn't hee-caw-haw, hee-caw-haw?" Noah asked between his guffaws.

She wanted to be mad, and she was fairly certain he wanted her to lash out at him. They'd had their fair share of arguments as children, many times resulting in her stomping away from him in a huff. But she wasn't a child anymore. She was a grown woman, and there were other ways to get back at him for teasing her. Like making sure he didn't get a bite of the jalapeno apple pie she'd brought with them. She was about to say as much, too, but he slowed the buggy and they turned down his parents' driveway. "Look, Jacob," she said, pointing at the large farmhouse with the wraparound porch where she'd spent so much time with her family and his. "Your *grossmammi* and *grossdaddi*'s *haus*."

Jacob lengthened his spine and moved to stand for a better look. His chubby fingers gripped the dash of the buggy. "Ah, ah."

He looked up at her as if to gain her approval. Instead of shaking her head or telling him no, she said, "*Grossmammi. Grossdaddi. Mammi. Daddi.*"

"Ammi. D-d." He grinned up at her, the warmth of his enthusiasm filling her heart in places she didn't know had holes.

She nodded. "*Gut* job, Jacob."

Noah brought the buggy to a halt and set the brake. He jumped down from the buggy as if he was a youth, like one of her younger brothers, and then reached for Jacob. He put Jacob on his feet and patted his straw hat. "Go see *Ammi* and D-d."

She was still irritated with his teasing, but her heart swelled by leaps and bounds at Noah's use of Jacob's language. Eventually, he'd have to encourage Jacob to use the correct words at the best of his ability. For now, Noah's journey into his *sohn*'s world showed her he was willing to learn how Jacob communicated, and that meant so much to her. Was he beginning to believe in his son? In her? Noah turned toward her and held out his hand. Her heart fluttered in her throat. It was one thing to take a buggy ride, quite another for their hands to touch. They'd held hands in the past, but as children playing games. This was different.

"Are you ready?" he asked.

She rubbed her dry lips together. "*Jah.*"

He searched her eyes. "I should warn you, they're not expecting you."

"You always were one for surprises." She took his hand and scooted across the bench. He didn't let go as she stepped down, forcing her to look up at him. His tall, broad frame shielded her from the sun. She was struck by how he'd grown into such a handsome man.

"*Denki*," he said, seemingly ignoring her comment.

She blinked, surprised by his quick change of topic.

"What you have done, what you're doing with Jacob, it's *wunderbar*," he said. "I think we can renegotiate our agreement. Maybe extend it through the summer until you go back to work when school starts again."

The skin on her forehead bunched together. "You didn't have to bring me to your parents to ask me that."

"No," he said. "I didn't have to, but I wanted to find a way to say thank-you for what you have done. Not just for my *sohn*, but for me, too."

"I didn't do anything special," she said.

"Maybe not, but in a few short days you opened my eyes to a world of possibilities with Jacob. You've shown me, with the help of your *mamm*'s wisdom, that hope is possible. I just need to reach out and take it. All I ask is you show me the same patience that you show Jacob. This is all new to me."

"I'm curious," she said as she started walking toward

his *mamm*'s house, pleased when Noah fell in step with her. She didn't want his family to speculate if they looked out the window and saw them taking their time. They might get the wrong impression. "How did *Mamm* open your eyes? I hope she didn't lay a guilt trip on you."

Lydia feared her mother was about to take a hint from Esther's book and play matchmaker.

"No, not at all. She talked to me about farming. And reminded me that when I plant seeds I never worry about whether those seeds will produce fruit. I know that they will. I don't worry about drought or floods, at least not until there is cause for some concern, and then faith carries me through until it's time to harvest. I'm grateful no matter how big or how little the outcome might be."

Lydia halted and glanced at him. "And how did that help you believe hope is possible?"

"Well, when I told her there was a difference between what you're doing with Jacob and what a farmer does when it comes to planting because one has been proven by experience. She reminded me just because I don't have experience with what you are doing doesn't mean you don't."

She was a little shocked that *Mamm* defended her in such a way when it came to her work with children. Especially when she'd often hinted that Lydia would regret it if she didn't settle down and marry soon. *Mamm* had never told her to quit working, and the money she earned helped around the house, plus Lydia was able to save some, but there was always that underlying pressure for her to marry someday soon, preferably before any of her younger siblings. But Lydia didn't have any interest in marrying, not when her heart had been set on one man for so long, only to have it broken by that same man when he asked her best friend to be his *fraa*. "*Denki* for sharing that. It's nice to hear my parents are supportive of me. I mean, I know they are, but to hear it is nice, *jah*?"

"*Jah*, both of your parents love you and think highly of your work with children. I know it's not our way, but are you going to one of those *Englischer* schools so you can be one of their teachers?"

She considered him a moment, wondering why he asked. Had he heard a rumor? Was he worried she'd leave Garnett? Before she could ask him about his question, the crunch of buggy wheels rolling up the drive stole her attention. She laughed. "Speaking of my parents, here they are."

Noah stepped back, placing a great deal of distance between them. A sense of rejection pricked her conscience, and she couldn't stop herself from analyzing his reaction. Did he fear her parents would make assumptions? Wasn't that exactly why she'd started walking toward the house, to keep his family from making assumptions? It wasn't like they were courting. She was just a friend helping a friend, keeping a deathbed promise she should have acted on long ago. "I guess Del told them I was here."

"*Jah*, I guess," he said. His shoulders slumped and he looked as if he'd eaten a sour apple. He turned back toward his buggy. "I'll grab your pie."

As his shadow moved away from her, a bit of sadness touched her. She'd been enjoying their conversation, one of the first genuine conversations they'd had in a long time. And there was no one to blame but herself for not continuing to be a good friend after Collette's death.

If Noah knew Lydia's parents and most of her siblings were going to visit his parents today, he probably wouldn't have invited her to dinner, and open them both up to speculation. He went in search of Lydia to get a break from all the curious glances and found her in the kitchen slicing a double layered white cake. "Jacob is entertaining Bridget and Alice with animal sounds, and they taught him a new one. Sheep."

"Oh, nice. I wonder if the Hochstetlers will let us come over so Jacob can see the sheep," she said. "I mean, if you don't mind."

"I don't mind," he said. "I didn't ask you here to cut cake." He dipped his finger into the thick white frosting.

She smacked his hand.

"Hey," he said.

"This isn't work, it's family," she said, focusing on stirring. "And just like everyone else, you need to wait until after we eat to have dessert."

He felt as if he'd been kicked in the chest. Ever since Collette's death, family had been a distant idea. Sure, he had his parents and his *bruders* and *schwestern*, but he hadn't felt as if he was a part of it all as he had before Collette's death. He hadn't had that connection without the cover of pity and disappointment for a long while, even before Jacob's condition was evident, but the last week he'd begun to have that connection again, and he owed it to Lydia.

Was bringing her here his way of trying to reform the bonds he once had with his parents and his siblings? He wanted to believe his parents were only disappointed in how life had turned sour for him, but he couldn't help wondering and really believing they were disappointed he hadn't better control over Jacob. That was a thought for another day, but he knew if he was strong enough, he'd ask his *daed.* He was just afraid of the truth.

Wanting to be free from the line of thoughts threatening to chase him back to isolation, he moved his finger toward the frosting.

"Noah Beiler, if you don't stop your fooling around, you won't get any cake," Lydia said as she scooted the cake stand out of his reach and placed herself between him and the cake. She held the plastic knife up as if to smack him with it like *Mamm* used to do when he was a boy.

He grinned at her and snatched the frosting covered knife. He jumped back when she tried to swipe it.

"Noah, give it back." She reached for it, and he stretched his arm high. "Please."

"What is going on in here?" His *mamm* appeared in the doorway, with her eyes narrowed and hands fisted on her hips, but he saw the twinkle in her eye, a twinkle he hadn't seen when speaking to him for a long time. "You know I don't like horsing around in my kitchen."

Lydia's *mamm* stepped close behind his *mamm.* "Are you two causing trouble again?"

"Again? I don't cause trouble. That's all Lydia." He gave a sheepish grin and handed the plastic knife back. "Here," he said. "You are all no fun."

Their mothers both walked through the kitchen with purpose. His *mudder* pulled another cake from the pantry, and Malinda lifted a large pitcher from a hook.

"I'll show you fun when you find rocks in your cake," Lydia tossed at him.

"Now, children, let's be nice. Noah, Alice and Bridget are wanting Talia to take them to go see the horses. Jacob is showing Elam and your *daed* how to make donkey sounds," Malinda said.

Noah flinched as a sense of urgency to rescue his father and Elam from his son overcame him.

"They're enjoying themselves," *Mamm* reassured him. "But Jacob's beginning to sound hoarse from all his hee-cawing. Did you forget about that lemonade you promised him?"

Noah's laughter received a glare from Lydia. "Our poor fathers are the recipients of Lydia's inability to make donkey sounds."

"Hush, Noah." Color heightened her cheeks, illuminating her eyes. He found her even more beautiful than he ever thought she'd been.

"Hee-caw-haw," he teased as he jumped back. This time he didn't miss her tap with the frosting covered plastic knife. He cleaned off a dollop from his forearm and licked it off his finger. "Yum."

"Go!" Lydia pointed at him. She feigned anger but he could tell by the twinkle in her eye and the smile teasing the corner of her mouth that she was having just as much fun as he was.

"Fine," he said. He opened his *mamm*'s propane refrigerator and pulled out a pitcher of cold lemonade before grabbing a small blue cup from the hutch. "Will you keep Lydia from putting rocks in my cake?"

"Your cake?" she huffed. "You're not getting any."

"We'll see about that," he said and left the kitchen, his cheeks sore from smiling too much, proving those muscles had found little use in recent years. It felt good to laugh and smile. Not just to laugh, but to feel joy in his entire being. And he owed that all to the woman who stood toe to toe with him.

Noah stopped dead in his tracks when he came around the corner of the wraparound porch. Jacob sat on his *daed*'s lap as he held his face in between his small hands. Noah couldn't remember the last time his father had been that close to Jacob, let alone enough to touch him.

"I have lemonade," Noah said as he set the pitcher on the folding table and poured some in a cup. Jacob kissed his *grossdaddi*'s cheek and then scrambled off his lap. "I hope he hasn't been any trouble."

Noah still couldn't believe the affection his child was sharing with his *grossdaddi*. Seeing the two bond, even if it was just for this moment, swirled a great deal of an unnamed feeling in his chest, and he had to fight back the overwhelming emotion. It brought to mind the days when he sat on his own *grossdaddi*'s lap as he told Noah stories about the kind of games he'd played as a boy. And the tall farming tales. His grandfather had liked to grow watermelons in *Grossmammi*'s garden to see if his melons outgrew his neighbors'. He was glad he'd witnessed the sweet moment between his *daed* and Jacob. It was a memory Noah would hold near to his heart until he took his last breath.

"Oh, no, he was no trouble. Not at all," *Daed* said. "We've had quite the interesting conversation."

"*Gut*," Noah said as he helped Jacob climb onto a lawn chair, and then he motioned *please* just as he'd seen Lydia do. "Drink, please."

Jacob tilted his chin. His blond little eyebrows rippled, and Noah felt the coming explosion deep in his gut. He was fully aware of Elam and his *daed* watching them.

He knelt in front of his *sohn*. "Jacob," he said, signing *please*. "Please."

The corners of Jacob's mouth turned upward, and Noah's pulse skittered. He had a sense of standing in the hayloft, his toes at the edge of the hay gable as he pitched bales to the wagon below. Heights terrified him, and he tried not to think about tumbling to the ground if he lost his balance. He just had to remember to keep knees slightly bent and his feet planted.

He pulled in a breath, squared his shoulders, and held out the cup as he signed again. "Jacob, please."

"P—p—please," Jacob said, his toothless grin spreading ear to ear.

The tension in Noah's shoulders released. He handed the cup to his son. "*Gut*, Jacob. Very *gut*."

Jacob busied himself with inspecting the inside of his cup. Noah sat in the chair beside him, thankful his son's tantrum was diverted.

"I'm impressed," his *daed* said.

"*Denki*," Jacob said, nodding.

"I am, too, Noah," Elam said, his eyes twinkling. "Now tell us how it's going in the kitchen."

"I was kicked out," Noah said, feigning innocence.

Elam chuckled. "I learned long ago it's best to stay out of the kitchen when the ladies are getting ready to serve dinner."

Noah hadn't had the luxury of having ladies in his kitchen of late, and Collette hadn't been the type to tease. Of course, he didn't cook much, just canned soups and sandwiches. Thankfully, Jacob didn't mind most of the foods they ate, and preferred peanut butter and jelly sandwiches. "I'll have to remember that. It's dangerous in there."

"By the look of the white frosting on your cheek, you tried to sneak a bite," his *daed* teased.

Noah reached up to wipe his face. "Lydia threatened to put rocks in the cake."

"Is that all?" Elam asked. "I recall Malinda dumping cayenne pepper in a pie once after I accidentally cut down one of her hydrangea bushes. She had reminded me where it was. Guess I didn't pay close enough attention. I never forgot after that."

Noah burst out laughing. "You can't be serious?"

"I am, and I can tell you, I'm thoroughly aware of where Malinda has planted all her perennials, and I keep my distance. Beachy women can be dangerous and will exact revenge in the most interesting ways. But I can say I've never been bored since the day I married Malinda. She keeps me on my toes."

Daed guffawed. "I can say the same about the Graber women. Your *mamm* keeps me on my toes, for sure and for certain, Noah. Never a dull moment."

"Remind me to never marry a Beachy or Graber woman," Noah said.

"Be careful what you say, *sohn*," his *daed* said. "*Gotte* has a way of bringing situations into our lives when we decide it's not for us."

"Good thing I've been married once. I don't need another *fraa*."

Both older men gave him looks of disbelief.

"You'll want more *kinner*," Elam said.

Noah shook his head. "I don't think so. I have my hands full as it is."

"Man was not meant to be alone, *sohn*," his *daed* said.

Noah leaned forward and rested his elbows on his knees. "If that was true for me, then why was it *Gotte*'s will to let Collette die?" he asked in a whisper.

He was met with silence for a moment, and then his *daed* said, "Perhaps because His plans for her were to bear you a beautiful child."

He glanced at Jacob. His *sohn*, the child not of his blood, but of his heart, even though he challenged him at every end. He was thankful for his child, more than anyone could ever know.

"And maybe," Elam said, drawing Noah's attention back to him, "He has bigger plans for you and Jacob."

Noah snorted. "Our plans don't consist of much outside of the farm." And even the farm was limited.

"You need your community," his *daed* said.

The warm summer breeze cooled his bare forearms and ruffled the hair at his nape. In the heat of the day, a chill raced up his arms. The thought of subjecting Jacob to ridicule didn't set well with him. He wanted his son to be accepted, even if he didn't understand the feeling. He chastised himself. Who was he to say what Jacob understood and what he didn't? Certainly not him. Which was just as good a reason as any to keep his child shielded from disdain.

"My community doesn't want my *sohn* as he is, and we're a package deal."

"They don't understand him, but given time," Elam said, "they will, and they'll see the gift he is."

"I'm just now beginning to understand him," Noah responded, knowing he owed that to Lydia.

"All parents need time to get to know their children

and grandchildren and understand them, Noah." His *daed* folded his hands in his lap. "I'm still trying to understand your *schwester*."

Noah chuckled. "I agree, she is a puzzle at times."

"Don't let her hear you say that, or she might do more than put rocks in your cake," *Daed* teased back. "Your *mudder* understands Talia well enough, and she helps me understand your *schwester* when she leaves me scratching my head. I do owe you an apology. Talia bent my ear last night and made me see the error of my ways where Jacob is concerned. I realize he may need more understanding than the rod."

Noah didn't know what to say. "*Denki.* Talia will make a *gut fraa*."

"*Gut* helpmates are hard to find, Noah," Elam added. "Your *mamm* and *daed* complement each other when it comes to raising children. Just as Malinda and I complement each other." Elam took on a faraway gaze, and he leaned against the back of his lawn chair. "I wouldn't have made it through Delphine's ordeal without sinning if it wasn't for Malinda's tender heart and cool head. She had the strength and courage to check my temper and keep me from causing harm to another man when that's all I wanted to do."

Somewhere in the distance, the horses neighed. Alice's and Bridget's giggles rolled across the lush green lawn. There was a time Lydia, all her sisters and his would stroll out to the field and offer their hands to scratch the noses of his *daed*'s attention-seeking horses. How had they all managed to find happiness when their sister would never walk again? How did they manage their day-to-day lives knowing Delphine was limited by a wheelchair?

"I am sorry for what you went through, Elam," Noah said. "For what you're going through. It can't be easy watching Delphine's life not turn out as you and Malinda had hoped."

"*Denki*," Elam said. "Malinda keeps me balanced. A *gut*, strong and capable Amish woman would do that for you, too, if you gave her a chance."

"He's right, Noah," his *daed* said. "You don't have to raise Jacob alone. You have willing family and friends to help. You have a community."

You have Lydia. The thought entered his mind without his permission. He couldn't have Lydia, not as anything more than a teacher, to help him learn from his son. Not when he feared it was his fault for Collette's illness and death. Even though he'd been honest with Collette from the very beginning of their courtship about his feelings for Lydia, he still couldn't help blaming himself for her death.

Chapter Ten

Lydia carried a plate of hot corn on the cob outside and took in all the activity. *Daed*, Silas, and Isaiah had returned home and brought back Delphine. It was quite the sight seeing her sitting in the truck bed *Daed* pulled behind the tractor. Silas and Isaiah sat on either side of her in their lawn chairs to keep her from tipping over.

It'd been a long time since the Beachy family and the Beiler family had gathered, and it felt good.

She set the plate of corn on the table and caught a glimpse of Noah in the side yard, helping Jacob hold a bat. Remmy wheeled his arm backward and then forward as he released a baseball in a slow arching pitch. Jacob's little arms lurched forward as Noah guided them to swing. The white ball sank to Jacob's feet. Pauly said something she couldn't hear but she noticed how Jacob stepped back and let him pick up the ball. Her youngest brother tossed it back to Remmy, and then said something that made both Noah and Jacob smile.

She loved watching father and son together. She'd do just about anything to preserve this moment.

Remmy repeated his slow pitch. The moment the ball sailed over the stick home plate, Jacob's swing connected. The ball thudded and dropped a few feet in front of him.

Lydia's heart jumped into her throat, and she clapped. "Run, Jacob, run!"

Kliem, Noah's *daed*, jogged from first to second. Delphine wheeled her chair outside the baseline, waving Bridget from second to third. "Go, go, go!"

Silas picked Bridget up to keep her from touching the base. Noah snagged Jacob by the waist and hitched him to his side as they ran to first base, marked by a feed sack. Alice stretched her hand out as Pauly tossed the ball. Noah settled Jacob on the feed sack the moment Alice snatched the ball.

"Safe," her *daed* yelled.

"Yay!" Lydia jumped up and down, clapping.

"What are they doing?" Jessie asked as she placed a bowl of cut watermelon and a bowl of potato salad next to the corn.

"Playing ball." Lydia's face hurt from smiling.

"Do you think *mamm* would mind me playing?"

She glanced down at her sister, part woman, part child, and recalled what it had been like to be her age. She'd be thirteen soon, and with only having two more years of school left, her sister's youth would be exchanged for learning how to become a wife and mother. Lydia had embraced the change into womanhood with the enthusiasm of a puppy with its first taste of a meaty bone. But looking back, she wished she would have dragged her feet a little more. "Go, Jessie, have fun. I'll finish setting the tables."

"*Denki*," Jessie said, wasting no time running toward the makeshift ballpark.

"They're having fun," Talia said, coming up from beside her with a couple plastic covered containers.

"They are," Lydia agreed. "They all are."

"I knew the time you spent with Jacob and Noah was good, but look at them," Talia said. "I haven't seen them like this. Ever. I mean, I've never seen Jacob play, not like this. And Noah is right there with him. What you have done is *wunderbar*."

"I had nothing to do with this," Lydia said. "This is all Noah and Jacob."

If Noah had told her she could no longer work with Jacob, bearing witness to their families having fun together today was enough. Seeing Jacob run and play like a child should, and seeing the shadows gone from Noah's eyes, was enough. Thankfully, he'd given her the rest of the summer.

"Is there more to bring out?" Lydia asked.

"Actually," Talia said, "*Mamm* asked me to trade places with Noah so he could carry the roasting pot off the stove. Oh, and your *mamm* wants you to go in and grab the applesauce and cottage cheese from her."

"*Denki*," Lydia said. She took one last look at the baseball game, longing to join in, but knowing it was wise to keep her distance. Something *Mamm* had said had propelled Noah to extend her offer through the end of the summer, and she couldn't tell him no, even though a big part of her heart had wanted to run as far and as fast away from him as she could. Seeing the freedom Noah had with his child and with their families healed parts of her heart that had been broken since Collette's diagnosis, but she needed to keep in mind the guilt she still carried.

She turned toward the house and trudged up the steps, her heart heavy once again. Collette should be here, watching her family and finding joy in their ball game, not Lydia.

The screen door screeched open.

Mamm smiled at her. "I'm almost finished with the garnishes. Can you grab the tomatoes and cucumbers from our basket?"

Lydia nodded. She pulled the containers from the basket, and then stacked the bowls of cottage cheese and applesauce on top. "I sent Jessie to play baseball. She should be a child for as long as possible, *jah*?"

"Of course, she should," Pearl, Noah's *mamm*, said. "There's no need to rush into adulthood, not during the summer. Especially on Sundays. Days of rest and play."

Now that she was becoming an old maid, according to Gideon and Esther, Lydia wished she wouldn't have spent so much time mooning over a boy who thought of her as nothing more than a friend, and she wished she'd spent more time playing, too. But when she'd been thirteen, fourteen-year-old Noah had been at the front of her thoughts.

"I agree," *Mamm* said. "The child has had a time of it lately. I never know if she'll be laughing or crying from one moment to the next."

Lydia pulled in a breath and sighed. "A first crush will do that."

"At least you had Delphine, and Bridget will have Alice. Poor Jessie is surrounded by *bruders*."

"Speaking of crushes, I ran into Trudy at the market two days ago," Pearl said.

Lydia gritted her teeth and waited for the gossip about her to meet her ears. However, since she'd never crushed on Gideon, she wasn't too concerned about what Trudy might have told her. She just hoped Pearl and her *mamm* didn't bring up Noah. Even though she'd never told anyone besides Collette and Delphine that she had liked Noah, she was sure their mothers had known. How could they not, the way Lydia had followed him around?

"I know it's none of my business, but I think of you like a daughter... Are you and Gideon courting again?"

Again?

"I always wondered why you two broke it off the first time."

The first time. What was Pearl talking about? She glanced at her *mamm*, who shrugged, and then back to Noah's *mamm*.

"I know it's our way to keep courtship quiet, but I thought as close as our families were, you would have told us," Pearl said.

"I'm not sure I understand. There has never been anything to tell," Lydia didn't know what to say or how to respond. She'd gone from the high of seeing Noah and Jacob freely playing to the low of knowing she had to put some distance between them before she gave any more of her heart to the father and son. Being the subject of gossip was like walking unexpectedly through a cocklebur patch barefoot. Especially when it came to Gideon Yoder. They'd been friends, just like Noah and Collette had been friends, until the night Gideon gave her a ride home. She'd been uncomfortable with his conversation and insinuations. She'd been thankful when he'd turned his attention elsewhere. Even if she hadn't had a crush on Noah back then, she still wouldn't have been interested in Gideon. He was too aggressive. Not in a physically abusive way, but rather in a demanding, determined way. He expected most people to line up with his opinion, and

Lydia was too strongheaded to bow to that kind of pressure. "We have never courted," she said.

And now, wondering if Gideon had alluded to Trudy more than was true, she'd have to quit standing on the fence and give him a definitive no.

"I think I'll take these dishes out to the table," Lydia said as she walked out the door, determined to get her name out of the gossip loop. It wasn't their way, and she didn't like that people were crossing boundaries with her name on their lips.

As she approached the table seeing Noah walking toward her, her heart lodged in her throat. She found herself crushing on him, maybe even more than she had eight years ago when she'd prayed and longed for him to ask her to court him. That rejection no longer hurt, but by the reaction in her limbs and pulse, if she didn't put up some emotional walls and quickly, her heart would shatter when summer came to an end. She needed something else to focus on besides Jacob and Noah. Something to look forward to.

Maybe she should reconsider going to an *Englischer* school to become a teacher. If she left the community, Noah wouldn't be a problem for her anymore.

"It was a *gut* day, *jah*?" Noah spoke in hushed tones to keep from disturbing his sleepy *sohn* as he drove her home.Another few minutes, and his child's blue eyes would lose the fight to stay open.

Lydia nodded, the waning sunlight catching the firm line of her mouth. She'd been quiet since she had brought the covered dishes out to the table, and he wasn't sure why. Instead of chatting with him and keeping him company, she'd wandered across the yard without a word and focused on some object in the field. Had something happened?

"Is everything okay?" he asked, over the draft horses' hooves.

She nodded. Again. The pale silhouette of her face against the evening blue sky, streaked with pinks and purples, barely moved, but he saw it. She rubbed her lips together and breathed deeply. He couldn't help noticing the shudder on her exhale.

Pulling on the reins, Noah brought the buggy to a halt, draped his arm across the back of the seat and touched her shoulders. Lydia snapped a wide-eyed gaze at him. "What?"

His pulse thundered in his veins. There was so much he wanted to tell her but couldn't. Like how he'd waited for a moment like this since they'd been youth driving home from a singing. But if he told her that, she'd want to know why he had never asked her before. And that was something he could never tell her. Which was one reason why he could never pursue a relation with her outside what they currently had—a friend who was helping his son.

He gripped the reins tightly, and considered saying *never mind*, but he had never seen Lydia like this, sullen and contemplative. He and Collette had told each other everything—she'd known his deepest secret and he'd known her darkest one—but they'd been more friends than anything. There was nothing at stake between them. No lost love, or friendship. Fear of conversation had never touched him with Collette, not until her diagnosis. Then he'd kept his thoughts to himself. He'd never known what to say, especially when *sorry* seemed too small of a word against such a life-changing disease.

"Something is wrong," he said, swallowing down his hesitation.

"No, it's not," she said. "It's been a long day, *jah*?"

He glanced in the mirrors to make sure an *Englischer* car didn't approach and then rolled the tension from his neck. "Did *Mamm* say something that upset you?"

Her pause told him all he needed to know, but she kept her lips clamped tight.

"I understand if you don't want to tell me," he said. "I would apologize, but I don't know what I'm apologizing for. I am sorry she said something that has caused you to be sad, though." He flicked the reins and moved them up the road toward her *haus*. "I only hope whatever was said, it won't stop you from visiting Jacob."

Lydia shook her head. "No, of course not."

Noah breathed a sigh of relief. At least that was something. Lydia would still come over. He wasn't sure why that settled peace within him, except today had been a *gut* day. Jacob hadn't had one tantrum. Yesterday had been a different story.

"I don't think anything could stop me from working with Jacob, unless you asked me to, or unless you remarried."

Air hissed through his teeth. "I don't think that will happen."

His *daed* and Elam had put the fear in him of having more *kinner*. He wasn't sure how he could manage another and Jacob. Besides, Jacob was enough for him. "Can I ask you a question?" Now that she was talking instead of stewing, he felt it was safe enough to press forward.

"I'm not stopping you, but I may not have an answer," she said, sounding more like herself and less like the sullen woman who'd left his *mamm*'s kitchen after helping clean up.

"Why haven't you married yet?"

Silence held them for a moment, and he glanced down at his son curled into Lydia's side. His dark eyelashes rested against his chubby cheeks, and his breath rose and fell in an even cadence.

"I haven't found the right man worth giving up my job for."

It was an honest answer. "I know it's none of my business, but many of our friends have married by now."

"Oh, there are a few holding out," she said, wrapping her arm around Jacob.

The hitch in her voice made it impossible for Noah to gauge her emotion.

Was she offended by his statement, or had she found it funny? "Does our conversation bother you?"

"No," she said, shaking her head, and then she sighed. "Actually, yes, but not because of you. Because my age and my lack of a *mann* and *kinner* seems to concern many people lately. What if I want to take after your Aunt Esther and remain unmarried? She's done just fine, as far as I can tell."

Noah laughed. "Because she is well loved by all her nieces and nephews."

"And you think I won't be?" she asked. "I'll have you know, I'll be the best *aenti* in Garnett."

"I'm sure you will, but seeing you with Jacob, you'd be a great *mamm* too. You're good with him. Patient."

She glanced over at him, and he saw something akin

to pain flicker in her eyes, but it was quickly gone. "I'd be just as content being an *aenti*. I mean, look at Esther. Her heart is full."

"Some of us are jealous that Malachi has monopolized her for so long, but honestly," he said, and then paused to gather his words. "I'm not sure I could do her and Jacob justice if she lived with me."

"Noah," Lydia said. She reached across Jacob's body and touched the back of Noah's hand. "You don't give yourself enough credit. You are strong and capable, but sometimes you're too stubborn for your own good." She took a breath, and he knew she was considering her next words. "If you take away nothing else from my time working with Jacob, please understand that it's okay to ask for help. Your family loves you, and they only want the best for you and your *sohn*."

He hoped so, but it was hard to trust when he'd been met with a lot of barriers. "I will try. I have to admit, today opened my eyes to the possibilities. And Jacob even said please. It was scary for a moment, if I'm going to be honest. I thought he might have a tantrum, and feared my *daed* would demand I spank him. But my *daed* and I had a *gut* conversation, and I really tried to reinforce behaviors I've seen Jacob do with you."

"That is *gut*, Noah, very *gut*," she said, and he felt himself respond to her praise. He was certain he was smiling like Jacob did when Lydia gave him praise. "Celebrating the wins, even the small ones, will go a long way through the hard days."

"*Denki* for being willing to have patience with my *sohn* and with me."

"Of course," she said. "And what about Collette's family? Have they not been around?"

He stiffened, putting slight tension on the reins. The draft horses jerked their heads, and the buggy slowed. Noah loosened his grip, and the buggy rolled forward. He didn't know how to respond. The moment they'd discovered Collette was pregnant, they'd shunned her, leaving him to pick up the pieces as any good Amish friend should. "Once we married, they had nothing to do with her or Jacob."

"Why is that, I wonder?" Lydia mused. "I always thought it was strange they didn't even go to your wedding."

It was only strange to her because she didn't know what he knew, but that was a secret he'd promised to keep. For the sake of his *sohn* and Collette's memory.

Noah turned the buggy up the drive leading to Lydia's *haus*. The moment fell far short of what he'd thought his first buggy ride with her would be, but it was also so much more. Although he sensed she erected a wall between them, others had fallen, and for that he was grateful. He only wished he could tell her the truth. If he hadn't made a promise to Collette when they'd married, he'd be free to marry again. But he wouldn't dishonor Collette's confidence, not even in death.

"Will we see you tomorrow?" he asked as he pulled the reins and set the brake.

"Yes, after my chores, and Delphine's. Seems I owe her."

"It was good to see Delphine playing ball, too," he said, feeling the warmth of family and friends they'd shared throughout the day. He stepped down from the buggy and picked up Jacob from the bench so Lydia could get out. He reached his hand out to help her down. The contact sparked through him. Another time he could have pursued his interest in her, but it seemed *Gotte* had other plans for him.

"Yes, it was good to see everyone playing ball, Noah," she said, smiling up at him. "Even you and Jacob. Community is good for the heart and soul." She pulled her hand from his and he immediately felt the loss of her warmth. "Tomorrow, Noah."

"Tomorrow," he said, knowing the night would be long, filled with thoughts of how different his life could have been if he could have married Lydia. He pulled a blanket from beneath the seat and laid it on the bench to cushion Jacob, and then climbed back into the buggy. Daylight had almost been lost to him, but it would give him time to think and consider all the wise words from the day. Elam said a good helpmate would help bear the burdens he carried. Noah knew Lydia was strong enough and courageous enough, but could he marry her while withholding the secrets he kept buried in his heart? Could he keep the truth from her? He didn't think so, but he couldn't break his promise to Collette, either.

Chapter Eleven

Lydia waited until bedtime and collapsed on her bed, buried her face into her pillow and screamed. It was the only thing she could think to do after the day left her heart heavy and weary. She didn't want her parents to know she was feeling discontent.

"What is wrong with you?" Delphine asked.

How could she explain to her sister all the thoughts bouncing around in her head? The gossip about her and Gideon, her feelings for Noah that she had to deny, even to herself, keeping her promise to Collette while keeping her distance from the man who was once again stealing her heart. The fact Noah had brought up marriage. Not between them. Not in a romantic sense, but out of curiosity. And for some reason that bothered her.

She propped up on her elbow and glared at Delphine through the kerosene lamplight. Her sister lay on her back with her hands curled under her chin. The quilt *mamm* made for her in shades of pink and yellow lay across the end of the bed. Lydia would offer to cover her up when she turned the lamp off. "Why are we still sharing a room? Why aren't you sharing a room with Jessie?"

"Because you're my favorite *schwester*. Besides, once you marry, I'll have a room all to myself."

"That is your motivation for me to get married? Your own room?" Lydia sat up and let her legs hang off the edge of the bed. "I'm never getting married, but if I ever move out on my own, I'll make sure to put a bug in *Mamm*'s and *Daed*'s ears that it would do Jessie's maturity good to share a room with an older sister."

"You wouldn't," Delphine said.

"I would," she said. "There will be plenty of room and then Alice and Bridget wouldn't have to share a bed."

Del sighed. "Point taken. Now, tell me what's really going on?"

Lydia sighed, slumping her shoulders. "A lot, but let's start with Gideon Yoder."

Delphine's eyebrows arched, and she used her arms to push herself up and lean against her headboard. "Not Noah?"

"No. Well, yes, and Jacob and my promise to Collette, but mostly Gideon. Do you know Pearl asked me if we were courting?"

Delphine laughed.

"Aaaagain!"

"What?"

"Yes. It appears she's under the impression Gideon and I were courting several years ago. How or why would anyone ever think that?"

"Oh, Lydia," Delphine said as she patted the bed beside her. "Let me give you a sisterly hug."

Lydia slid off her bed and padded to her sister's. She climbed in beside her, resting her head on Delphine's shoulder. "If Pearl thought I was courting Gideon, did Noah think that, too? Did Collette? Is that why their courtship came out of the blue and he married her?"

She didn't wait for Del's response but instead broke into a torrent of tears. Her sister held her, allowing her tears to soak her shoulder.

"There now, Lydia. I'm sorry," Delphine said.

"Was it all a misunderstanding or did someone spread gossip about me that wasn't true?"

"Does it matter?" Delphine asked. "What's done is done, but if it was a misunderstanding, maybe you should tell Noah."

Lydia shook her head. "I can't. Like you said, what's done is done. And I fear Noah still grieves Collette. A love that holds on like that is hard to compete with. Besides, I don't want to be any man's second choice. Not Gideon's. Especially not Noah's."

"Why does it need to come down to being a second choice? Can't a man love more than one woman in his life if a man is left a widower? Can't a woman? What about April? She was a widow and fell in love with Malachi."

"That is different," Lydia said. "She didn't know Malachi before meeting her first husband. I've known Noah and Gideon all my life and they chose others over me."

"You know you're my favorite sister, *jah*?" Delphine drew her fingers through Lydia's hair.

Lydia sniffled. "You say that now, but tomorrow it'll be Jessie."

"Let's not be foolish Lydia. Jessie will never be my favorite. At least not for a week," Del teased.

"All right, Bridget then. What's your point?"

"You overthink things too much, you make it hard and you allow fear to steal what joy you could have. There, I said it."

"You know how much it broke my heart when Collette and Noah married. I had to be happy for them. I had to pretend, and so much bitterness festered in my heart. I don't know if I could survive the bitterness a second time around if I allowed my heart to break again. I fear jealousy."

"Who says your heart will get broken if you open it up to try?"

"Who says it won't?"

"I guess we'll never know if you don't try," Delphine said. "Isn't that something like what you told Noah about Jacob?"

"I don't know, Del." Lydia pulled away from her sister and folded her hands in her lap. "We're talking apples and oranges."

"Are we?"

Lydia considered her sister's honest question. "One is about redirecting behaviors and educating parents on how to help prevent them. True, the process doesn't work every single time, but mostly it does, until it doesn't. But it's a process—"

Delphine touched her arm. "Lydia, you're rambling."

Shuddering, Lydia scooted to the edge of the bed and let her feet drop to the floor. She was weary. Tired of her own emotions warring within her. "Don't tell *Mamm* and *Daed* yet, but I'm considering going to an *Englischer* school to become a teacher."

"You're going to leave the community?"

Hearing Delphine voice the consequence of her choice aloud rocked through her. A chasm of pain split her heart, and tears gathered on to her lashes and rolled down her cheeks. She loved her community. Every one of them. Even Trudy Smucker. The people she shared her life with were her heart and soul. Her breath. Community was so important to her well-being that the thought of anyone else being on the outskirts, like Noah and Jacob, caused her a great deal of stress. Could she leave? How could she convince Noah he needed the community to help him support Jacob if she was going to leave?

Lydia shook her head as she swiped at her tears. "I haven't decided."

She felt Delphine's hand touch her shoulder. "Why? Why would you leave us?"

The pain in her sister's voice struck another nerve, and the tears seemed to stream faster. "I don't know, Del. It just seems to be the right course of action for my life. I can do so much good."

"But you're doing good here, too. You don't have to have an *Englischer*'s certificate to keep doing what you're doing here in Garnett. If you did, they wouldn't have hired you at the school."

"I know, Del," she said as she slipped off her sister's bed, padded to hers and turned down the lamp. She threw back the blankets and crawled inside.

"I don't understand," Del said. The sound of clothing rustling against the sheets told Lydia her sister was getting herself settled for sleep.

Lydia didn't, either. "It just makes sense, Del. It just makes sense. Besides, it's too hard here."

"Too hard?" Del's sharp, angry tone reverberated through the dark. "Try being paralyzed."

The words struck Lydia like lightning. "Oh, Del, I'm sorry," Lydia said, jumping out of bed and back into her sister's. She climbed in next to Delphine and wrapped an arm around her. "I didn't mean to be insensitive. There's just too much going on here. Too much confusion. Everyone has an opinion about what I should do. Gideon thinks I should marry him because I'm getting too old to have children. Esther thinks I should marry Noah—"

Delphine let out a little laugh. "Esther might have the right of it, you know?"

"No, she doesn't. Even if Noah was emotionally available, how could I marry him after he was married to Collette?"

"Do you remember when Collette came to tell you she was going to marry Noah?"

Lydia squeezed her eyes closed. "How could I forget?"

"I was there eavesdropping, like a good sister should," Del said.

Lydia smacked her hand. "How dare you?"

"I always did, whenever I could." Delphine's chest rose and fell. "I remember seeing the anguish in her eyes. She didn't want to hurt you."

"No, but she did, and she knew how I felt about Noah."

"Do you remember Collette saying she hoped one day you would understand?" Delphine asked.

"No," Lydia said, but she remembered Collette holding her hand, saying those same words just a few days before she'd died. *I'm sorry for hurting you, Lydia. I'm sorry for marrying Noah. Not everything is as it seems, and I hope one day you will understand. When I'm gone, promise you'll take care of Jacob and Noah. They'll need you.* "I was angry and hurt. I saw nothing more than red the moment she told me she would be marrying Noah the next day. They didn't even have a proper courtship, and their marriage was so quick. Her parents weren't even there."

"Did you ever wonder why?"

"No," Lydia said. "I just assumed they'd had another priority that couldn't be helped, and that Collette and Noah had been courting when I wasn't around. Behind my back."

"That wasn't like Collette," Delphine said.

No, it wasn't. "I never would have believed she'd marry Noah either, but she did."

"Did you ever ask her why?"

"No," Lydia whispered into the dark. "I was too scared to know."

"And you're still too scared to know," Delphine said. "Else you wouldn't be running from Noah now."

"I'm not running. I've agreed to work with Jacob through the summer."

"You're thinking about leaving the community, Lydia," Del said. "You're giving yourself something else to focus on so you have an out."

Lydia climbed off her sister's bed, pulled the quilt up to Delphine's chin, and then crawled back into her own. "I am not."

But was she? Was she giving herself an out so her heart wouldn't get broken by Noah again? Would she be happy leaving the community? No, she wouldn't, but she wouldn't be happy living here once Noah fully integrated back in, not knowing she'd see him at church, and the market and at family dinners, because their families would have more gatherings together. Tonight was too much of a success to not do it again. At least if she went to the *Englischer* school, her life would have purpose, and that was something she could live with. At least she thought she could. Her mind made up, she allowed her eyes to quit staring into the dark and she drifted off to sleep.

* * *

Jacob stood at the screen door with his face smashed against the mesh. His first word upon waking was "D-d-d," and it warmed Noah's heart. It was *gut* for his *sohn* to take to another person, and after a long sleepless night, Noah was beginning to see Lydia's way of thinking about how the community could help him navigate Jacob's abilities.

Not just about the community, but about her, too. Which led him to wonder how she would respond if he asked her to court—not court, as they were too old, but he wanted to woo her like she deserved and then marry her. That thought had played in his mind more than he liked. It certainly didn't sit well with him, marrying her without her knowing the secrets he held, but he also didn't think he could fully enter the community without her. He didn't want to do it without her, and he wasn't sure how he could come to a resolution that would both honor his late wife and his need to tell any future wife the truth about his *sohn*.

Could he keep Lydia close without falling in love with her? He shook his head. He didn't think that was possible, because now he was certain he was already halfway there, and it wouldn't take much from her for him to jump fully into loving her.

The problem was Lydia would have questions about Collette's family. Just like she had questions last night, and those were questions he couldn't answer. He speared his fingers through his hair and growled. Jacob glanced up at him, his little blond eyebrows forming a deep V. "It's okay, Jacob. I'm *gut*. Jacob is *gut*, too, *jah*?"

His son nodded. "*Jah, jah.*"

His frustration over the promise Collette had asked him to keep to preserve her family's reputation was quickly overcome by wonder. Lydia had been right. Jacob was capable of more than he thought possible. It hadn't been that long ago that Lydia had shown up at his house with a basket of eggs and his son hadn't had a vocabulary, at least not one Noah understood. Almost three weeks since Lydia re-entered his life, four if he counted the day at the school, and today, Jacob was talking with his child and it wasn't completely one-sided. He knelt in front of Jacob and rested his hand on the child's shoulder. "I love you, Jacob. *Ich lieba dich, fashtay?*"

Jacob's bright blue eyes, framed by his dark eyelashes, stared at him.

"*Ich lieba dich,* Jacob," he repeated, only to receive a blank stare. "Always, Jacob, no matter what, you are my *sohn*. The child of my heart."

"D-d-d?" Jacob blinked.

"Yes, Lydia is coming today," Noah said, rising to his full height. "After her chores are done, she'll come. Would you like to go outside and wait?"

Before he could finish his question, Jacob rushed out the door. His little bare feet pattered down the steps. He stopped and turned toward the *haus* and waved at him to come. Noah smiled. Jacob definitely had a different language. His refusal to say *I love you* did not hurt Noah. He'd gotten used to that over the years, but a part of him hoped that maybe now, since Jacob was using his words, *I love you* would come.

He adjusted his suspenders onto his shoulders and followed behind Jacob. The moment he stood next to Jacob, his son smacked him on the leg and then took off running. "Me, me."

Noah burst into laughter, and pretended to chase after Jacob, always staying a bit out of reach so Jacob could get away. His son darted to the left, and then to the right. He giggled and snickered as he hid behind a tree, or the clothesline pole, all the while saying *me, me*. After a few minutes, to keep Jacob from getting too bored with the game, Noah tagged him. "Tag, you're it. You can't get me."

Noah tiptoed and fast-walked as Jacob chased him, eventually letting Jacob touch him.

"Agit," Jacob said, and Noah knew that he meant *tag, you're it*. He scooped his son into his arms and spun him in a wide circle. Jacob leaned his head back, and his smile seemed to touch the sky.

The sound of buggy wheels coming up the drive interrupted their play. Jacob pushed against his forearms, indicating he wanted down. Noah set him on his feet but held on to his shoulder to keep him from running toward the unfamiliar buggy.

Jacob pulled. "D-d."

"No," Noah said, shielding his eyes from the morning sun as he tried to discern who their most recent visitor was. "That's not Lydia. I don't know who it is."

His son's shoulders slumped, and Noah didn't like Jacob being disappointed. He'd give his son the sun and the moon if he could. The buggy drew closer, and Noah saw two people in the cab. One of them was his Great-Aunt Esther. Who was the other? It didn't look like his cousin, Malachi. Had Esther talked someone into bringing her out here?

The buggy rolled to a halt, and a man with a straw hat, white shirt with a dark vest and dark broadfall pants stepped down. He held his hand out for Esther. She shuffled toward them. Jacob quickly hid behind his leg, gripping the fabric.

"Hello, Aunt Esther," Noah said as he approached her. He reached his hand out for her and then kissed her soft cheek. "*Wie bischt?*"

"Oh, I am *gut*, very, very *gut*, now that I've seen my boys," she said. "And how are you?"

Glancing past Esther's shoulder, he watched the man unload a crate from the back of his buggy. "We are well," he said, and then reached for Jacob's hand. He knelt beside Jacob and lifted his chin to look him in the eye. "Jacob, this is Aunt Esther. She is my *grossdaddi*'s *schwester*."

Jacob glanced at Esther and then back to Noah. "D-d."

Noah shook his head. "No. Not your *grossdaddi*. *Aenti* Esther."

"It's nice to see you again, Jacob," Esther said as she bent over, removed Jacob's hat, and ruffled his hair. She looked between Noah and Jacob, her lips twisting in thought. "He doesn't resemble you, does he?"

Every nerve and muscle in his body went on full alert. Would his aging aunt, who suffered from memory slips and often didn't make sense, reveal his secret?

"I can't recall Collette enough to know who the child looks like. Never mind the musings of an old woman. Levi, bring the crate," she called back toward the buggy and then focused on Noah. "We've brought something for you."

Noah had just breathed easier after his aunt's perceptive gaze took in the blond-haired, blue-eyed little boy clinging to his pants, but grew nervous once again at what that something they'd brought for them might be. He'd heard stories about her recent mental confusion, but as Levi approached with the crate, his nerves settled a little. Surely Levi wouldn't have allowed Esther to bring something that would cause them trouble, would he?

"Cousin Noah." Levi dipped his head as he approached, carrying a crate lined with cardboard to cover the holes. Little peeps chirped from the container and warmth rocked through him at this gesture of kindness. Levi looked down at Jacob. "Cousin Jacob, would you like to see what I have in here?"

"Shall we go on the porch and out of the sun first?" Noah asked, seeing Esther was growing shaky and could use a chair.

Levi smiled. "*Jah*, it is a *gut* idea."

Noah held his arm out for Esther and allowed her to hold on to him. Jacob raced up the stairs and sat on the porch.

Levi chuckled. "Reminds me of Naomi's *bruders*. Always in a hurry, *jah*?"

"I think he's excited to see what is in the box," Noah said.

"As he should be," Levi said, from behind him.

"You are doing well, I see," Esther said as they climbed the stairs one slow step at a time. Her pace was on an entirely different spectrum than Jacob's. And he was fine with that. The slower pace was nice, and at least Jacob was sitting, even if he was rocking his little body while he anxiously waited.

"I am," Noah said, maneuvering Esther toward a chair.

"I'll grab another chair from the kitchen so we can all sit. It's not often we have company."

"No need," Levi said. "I will sit here next to Jacob."

"Are you sure?" Noah asked.

"Oh, yeah," he said as he started to pull the top off the box.

Jacob leaned forward, his eyes growing wide as he looked inside. He clapped his hands together and glanced at Noah. "Eeep, eeep."

"*Gut* job, Jacob," Noah said as he sat in the chair behind his *sohn*.

"Very *gut*," Esther said, and then she laid her hand on Noah's leg. "You need a *fraa*."

Noah's heart skipped a couple of beats. Levi's head fell forward, and then he rolled it up to look at Esther. "Aunt Esther, this is not why I brought you here. We discussed this. We came for a visit, nothing more."

His aging aunt lifted her chin. "I'm saying what I've got to say. I can't rest my body until you are well and married. That means you too, Levi."

Laughter rumbled from Noah's chest. After everything he'd heard about Esther's mental state, he was surprised to find her mind clear and focused. She was a little too outspoken for his comfort at the moment, but she did remind him a lot of another outspoken woman he couldn't purge from his mind. "Well, then, I'm glad I'm not the only one in your sights, Aunt Esther. You'll be pleased to know my *daed* and Elam Beachy had this very conversation with me only last night."

"Good sensible Amish men," Esther said with an ornery grin. "And?"

His cousin stuck his hand into the crate and pulled out

a little chick to show Jacob. Noah reached for his son's impulsive arms, just as Levi said, "It's okay, Noah."

Noah pulled back and watched his cousin and *sohn*.

"Soft, see, and gentle." Levi took Jacob's hand, opened up his curled fingers and drew them over the chick's downy feathers.

Jacob's face expressed the pleasure he felt at experiencing the baby chick. While his fingers continued to massage the chick's fur, Jacob leaned forward and looked into the crate.

"There are ten chicks. They're not ready for the coop just yet, maybe a few weeks. Elam said you purchased a new brooder and have the warming lights. Since I'm taking over Malachi's old *haus*, the chickens he left behind have been producing more eggs than I know what to do with. Malachi has kept a few for his own use, and I'll keep a few, but soon, I'll start breeding labradoodles, so I don't need them. There are more to come if you have the capacity and would like them."

Emotion tightened his chest. Lydia was right. He needed the community, and maybe, just maybe, he and Jacob could find a purpose for the community to need them, too.

"*Denki*," Noah said. "You humble me with your gift. I'm not sure how to repay you."

"No need," Levi said. "That's what family is for. Besides, there were many times you sheltered me and Abe when we were hiding from our stepdad. That's something we will always be grateful for."

"I only wish I could have done more."

"*Gotte* worked it out, *jah*? All is well, and even Abe came back, married and is settled where he should be."

"Now tell me about your labradoodles. Will you run it as a business, or keep them all?"

"Nephews," Esther said. "You cannot ignore me. I want to know what Noah has decided about marriage."

Noah had hoped she'd been distracted enough by the chicks that she had forgotten about the topic of marriage. He leaned his elbows on his thighs and held his aunt's discerning gaze. She might be losing her memory, but right now she appeared to be sharp as a tack. "I haven't, Aunt Esther. I have Jacob to consider, and there aren't many women who'd take on a child with his abilities. Not even an Amish woman."

"Oh, I think I know of one. She's perfect for the both of you," Aunt Esther said.

He chuckled, curious. "And who might that be?"

His aunt's grin was ear to ear, but it was broken by the sound of another buggy coming up the drive.

Jacob jumped to his feet and took off down the stairs. "D-d!"

Noah chased after him, but he was fairly certain he heard his aunt say, "I'm sure that's her now."

And for the life of him, he couldn't disagree. Lydia Beachy was probably the only woman he knew who would take on a widower and his difficult child.

Chapter Twelve

"D-d," Jacob squealed as he ran toward her.

She'd barely descended the buggy before Lydia had to prepare herself for the impact of his little body slamming against hers.

Her heart filled with an unknown emotion as he ran across the yard toward her, with his *daed* sauntering behind him. There was something pure and simple about seeing these two, and she had a flicker of a thought that if she could have this each day, her life would be perfect. But Noah was not her *mann* and Jacob was not her *sohn*.

She wrapped her arm around his back as he hugged her, taking delight in the joy he exuded at seeing her. "Hi, Jacob, it's *gut* to see you."

A shadow loomed over them, and she glanced up. She nearly became lost in Noah's dark brown eyes. "Hi."

"Hi," he said, his smile not quite reaching his eyes. "*Denki*, for coming."

"Of course," she said, quickly losing her confidence beneath the shadow of his darkened mood. Had something happened? If he'd changed his mind, he wouldn't have told her thank-you. She swallowed past the knot of fear in her throat that she'd somehow upset Noah, and that he would send her away, which was odd as she was considering leaving Garnett. She released Jacob, and he clenched on to her hand. She took delight at his little hand in hers. She glanced around the yard. "Has the morning been *gut*?"

"*Jah*, he's been anxiously, but patiently, waiting to see you." He smiled, his cheeks turning pink, and she breathed a sigh of relief. Jacob reached out his other hand for Noah, and they began walking toward the *haus*, the three of them together. She couldn't help the vision of them popping into her thoughts, like a family. The chasm she'd felt last night at the thought of leaving the community ripped through her again. This time, she kept her shock, grief and tears at bay. *We're just friends, nothing more.*

"That is *gut*. Progress, *jah*?" When he didn't respond, she rushed on to say, "You mowed. It looks *gut*."

His shoulders inched toward his ears. Although he had lost weight, he still looked handsome: broad shoulders, his forearms pressing against the roll of his shirtsleeve. "It wasn't me. Remmy mowed for me. Your *mamm* thought you might like to plant flowers with Jacob, so the flower bed hasn't been touched."

"Oh, *jah*, Jacob, would you like to help me plant flowers today?"

The child nodded.

"We have company," Noah said, sounding less than happy.

"I saw Esther and Levi when I parked the buggy by the barn," she said. When he didn't respond, she wondered if Esther was the reason for his mood. "That bad, huh?" she asked, only to receive a shrug.

Lydia was surprised to find Esther and Levi at Noah

and Jacob's. It was a *gut* surprise, but she was a little nervous given the slips Esther had experienced on Saturday. Lydia hoped Esther hadn't mentioned Collette, or Lydia being Noah's *fraa* as she had the other day. She hoped she hadn't mentioned marriage at all.

"Well enough," he finally said.

"I know you don't like company. I'm sorry. I should have warned you yesterday." She told him about the conversation between her and Esther on Saturday.

"It's not that." Noah shook his head. His locks curled longer than they should. He needed a haircut. "Levi brought chicks."

"Eeep, eeep," Jacob said.

Lydia covered her mouth with her free hand as she giggled. "That's right, Jacob. *Gut* job."

Jacob released her hand and Noah's and ran toward the porch where Esther and Levi sat.

"How has she been?" Lydia asked, curious to know if she was about to walk into one of Esther's own versions of her memories.

"*Gut*," he said. "But I'm guessing that's not what you really want to know." When he paused, Lydia feared the worst, but she kept quiet. "She's intent on marrying me off, and I believe you are the target."

"Oh!" Lydia stumbled over her feet but quickly righted herself when Noah reached and grabbed her elbow.

"Are you all right?"

"Yes, *denki*," she said as he released her elbow like he'd grabbed a pan from the oven without an oven mitt.

"I just thought you should know."

"I appreciate your honesty," she said, noting how his mouth turned down. "You could have let me walk in unaware. She's pretty vocal about her opinions. I'll tread carefully."

A shadow flickered across his eyes, and the crow's-feet at the corners kissed as his brow furrowed.

"At least she has *gut* taste, jah?" she teased, hoping to make him smile again. Her attempt fell short.

"She does," he said seriously. "But you'd be getting the short end of the stick, Lydia."

She stepped up two stairs, turned and looked over her shoulder. They were nearly the same eye level. Her breath hitched at the raw emotions pooling in his eyes. She thought to tease him, but what she saw gave her pause. "Don't sell yourself short, Noah Beiler."

"I could never be completely honest with you, Lydia."

She blinked, wondering what secrets he kept, and were they anything like hers? "We all have our secrets, Noah."

He tucked his thumbs into his suspenders as he shook his head. "That shouldn't be true between *mann* and *fraa*."

She pasted on a smile and turned to head up the rest of the stairs. "What a nice surprise, Esther, Levi. Jacob tells me you brought chicks."

She'd spent a long sleepless night running so many conversations through her head. Those with Esther on Saturday. Those with Noah yesterday when he'd asked why she'd never married, his *mamm* believing she was courting Gideon. She'd stopped by Trudy Smucker's house on the way over to drop off a pie in a show of good friendship and had reassured the younger woman she wasn't courting Gideon Yoder and had no interest in doing so. Of course, Lydia hadn't said it in such a direct manner, even if she wanted to, but had allowed it to drop in their conversation. Lydia had left there cheery and feeling as if her world was beginning to once again find balance because she knew it wouldn't take long for all of Garnett to know the truth about Lydia and Gideon. Including Gideon Yoder. But now, the strange conversation with Noah and his downtrodden demeanor had her feeling as if she was navigating a ship in the middle of the vast and stormy ocean without a rudder or a compass. Not that she'd ever had the occasion to be on a ship, or see the ocean, but she'd read the account of Jesus calming the storm and other books depicting such a scene in grave detail.

"*Jah*," Levi spoke. "Malachi and I have more than we need."

"See, Noah?" she said, smiling. "I told you family and community are important."

"Yes, you did," Noah said.

"Eeep, eeep," Jacob said, pointing inside the crate.

Lydia bent over and looked inside, then knelt beside Jacob. "Oh, look at them, Jacob. Soon they'll grow big and lay eggs. You like eggs, don't you?"

The child nodded his head.

"It'll still be about three months, and by that time it'll be late fall," Noah said.

Looking over her shoulder, she found Noah standing close behind her. "*Daed* has some mature hens for you and a *gut* rooster," Lydia said, standing. Noah stood so close to her she could smell the spearmint gum he liked to chew.

He searched her eyes as if he wanted to say something, as if something else was on his mind other than chickens and roosters. It was as if he'd forgotten Esther and Levi sat on the porch, too. He drew her into that moment, and she wanted to stand here suspended in time forever.

"They said they'll bring them over later today. Where are your *schwestern*?"

Her jaw fell slack. "Oh! I was so focused on my chores and getting here, I forgot to bring them." It wasn't a lie. She had been focused on getting here and seeing Noah. Knowing their time was coming to an end, whether she decided to tell him this would be her last week or if she remained until the end of the summer, she wanted to spend as much time with them as possible.

"Your *daed*?" he asked.

"It'll be fine. I think I'll go make some lemonade for everyone."

"No need on my account," Esther said, her words keeping Lydia rooted only a few inches from Noah. She wanted to lean into him, to feel his solid strength. "I know you have chores to tend to. I wanted to see with my own eyes how suitable you two are. They make a handsome couple, don't they Levi?"

"Aunt Esther, I think it's time to go," Levi said. "Lydia and Noah will marry who they want, when they want."

Lydia breathed a sigh of thanks for Levi's intervention.

"*Denki*, Levi," Noah said, voicing the thought in her head. "As I told my *daed* and Lydia's last night, I married once. I don't need to marry again."

"Like I said, *gut* sensible Amish men." Esther pushed up from her chair on shaky arms. Levi reached out to help her. "Wise, too. You should heed their advice. Come on, Levi, take me home, after we stop at the cafe for ice cream and apple pie."

Levi helped Esther down the stairs. "April won't like it."

"I'm an old woman. I can eat what I want."

Levi turned and waved. Noah gave his thanks, and Lydia said her goodbyes. They stood in silence beside each other, watching Levi's buggy until it disappeared down the drive while Jacob diligently watched the little chicks.

Lydia turned and blinked at Noah. "My father spoke to you about marrying?" she asked. No wonder Noah questioned her about why she hadn't married.

"Yes, but not about marrying you, just remarrying in general. They had a valid argument about how a *gut* helpmate would help bear my burdens."

"They meant Jacob," she said.

Noah nodded. "I believe so."

"They're not wrong," she said. "*Gut* helpmates can and do bear each other's burdens. I saw that with my parents after Delphine's accident."

"I know." Noah touched the tips of his fingers to hers. Her heart thundered in her chest. She could no longer dance around the edge of the past and what she once felt for Noah. She loved him, and his *sohn*. Probably more today than she thought she had as a young girl. It was too late to preserve her heart. She fought the tears burning the backs of her eyes. Realizing she was losing, she knelt back down by Jacob and pretended interest in the baby chicks.

It wasn't long before she heard his boots descend the porch stairs. She waited until she thought he was out of sight before wiping her tears.

Noah strode to the barn as fast as he could without running. What had he been thinking? He'd almost kissed her, just seconds before tears filled her eyes. He slammed the flat of his palm against his workbench.

"*Gotte*, what am I going to do?"

He loved Lydia. He knew that. He had long ago, and he did now but he couldn't offer anything more than friendship. Each moment they spent together pushed him closer to the edge of telling her what was in his heart. He pulled his straw hat off his head, tossed it onto the workbench and fell to his knees. He buried his face in his hands and sobbed.

If he could go back in time, would he change what he'd done? He shook his head. No, not even if it meant he could have courted Lydia and married her. He'd chosen his path when he'd helped a friend keep her dignity and remain within the community without getting shunned by the community. He'd taken responsibility for an action he hadn't committed. A grave sin. He'd never asked Collette what had happened or what the circumstances were, or even who Jacob's biological father was. All he knew was that she was in trouble and needed help.

He dropped his hands to his thighs and doubled over. What had his *daed* said about *Gotte*'s will for him and Jacob to have something better? What could that be? How could Jacob not having his mother be better for him? Because she wouldn't have been strong enough to care for him, not in the way Lydia did. He knew that in his heart, and truth be told, if he had courted Lydia and married her all those years ago, she would never have worked at the school and gained the experience of working with children like Jacob. It was almost as if *Gotte* had tailor-made Lydia to be Jacob's *mamm*. That still didn't resolve the issue of the promise he'd made to Collette. There was no way getting around that, and he wouldn't marry any woman if he couldn't tell her the truth about his *sohn*. He recognized the promise had been unfair of Collette to ask of him, but even when they knew she had cancer they'd never spoken about the vow. And when she was dying, he could have asked her to free him from the promise, but he was too caught up in his own guilt for not loving his wife as a *mann* should.

The truth was, he knew in his heart he couldn't keep going as he had. He'd seen Jacob flourish in the last week, and he'd just grow even more. Lydia had taught him how to enjoy his *sohn*. And even though they hadn't attended a church service or gone to the farmers market, he knew without a doubt Lydia would be the perfect helpmate to help him navigate those events with Jacob. She wasn't just perfect, she was the only one. Without her, he'd be lost.

He climbed to his feet. Now all he had to do was figure out a way to get out of the promise he'd made to Collette years ago, without breaking it. Maybe it was time to seek counsel. He couldn't seek it from his *daed*, as he was certain he would grill him until he knew the full truth. Elam was wise enough to provide him an answer, but he wasn't sure talking to Lydia's *daed* before speaking to her was a good choice on his part. Which left Bishop Mueller.

Noah let his head fall. The bishop's wife hadn't been kind to him about Jacob. Could he expect impartial advice from him? And if, in the conversation's course, the bishop discovered the truth about Jacob's true parentage, would he force the truth to come out to the *gmay*? Having his *sohn* labeled as an illegitimate child was not Noah's idea of a *gut* life for him.

Would he always be in between a rock and a hard place?

Noah swiveled on his heels, taking in the expanse of

the barn, looking for something, anything to give him a solution to his problem, but he came up blank.

He stepped outside. Lydia and Jacob were no longer on the porch but digging around in the flower garden. From his viewpoint, it looked as if they had already pulled weeds, and were filling the small bed with flowers. Jacob's smile told him he was happy with the task. He wandered toward the new coops and gave a prayer of thanks for Elam and Lydia's brothers. Without them, and Lydia, he'd still be wondering how to accomplish the task all while Jacob kept him busy. He turned around and headed back to the barn. The goats bleated at him, and he reached down and offered his hand for some scratching. Several of them pushed their way through for their turn, and he took the time to accommodate all eight of them. Three of them were about to have babies. Two of them were still producing milk from the previous kidding and he set out to milk them each day.

Goats, chickens and Jacob were about all he could handle at the moment. He turned his gaze toward the fallow field. A yearning to plow and plant called to him, but that was beyond his current abilities. Would Lydia agree to stick around after the school year began , at least on Saturdays and some evenings until he planted winter wheat?

Glancing back at the house, he saw Lydia and Jacob holding hands and walking toward her buggy. The flowers her *mamm* had brought over filled the flower bed and would fill in in a few weeks. Lydia opened the back of her buggy and pulled out a small cardboard box. Curious about what she had, Noah strolled across the yard.

"Here, let me," he said, taking the box from her. "Oh, what is this?"

"Mmm, mmm," Jacob said.

"It does look yum-yum," Noah said as he glanced at Lydia.

"I thought he might like some different jellies with his peanut butter," Lydia said.

"I don't think this is necessary." He picked up one of the jars out of the box. "He likes grape."

"And now he can have choices, *jah*?" Lydia said.

"I don't understand, Lydia. If we know he likes grape, why change?"

"If he doesn't know his options, how can he make informed decisions?"

She had a point.

"It's also another way of teaching him how to communicate. There are three different colors. I realize the blueberry is like his grape, but that will add to the challenge." She climbed the stairs, holding Jacob's hand. "Jacob, will you open the door for me, please?"

His *sohn* released Lydia's hand and opened the door. Lydia took the box from Noah, her eyes light and teasing. "I'd ask you to join us for lunch, but given I forgot to bring one of my *schwestern*, we best keep as separated as possible. You should get the chicks settled in their new home. We'll make you a sandwich if you'd like."

"It's a *gut* thing you won't forget a sister tomorrow, right?" he teased.

"And a *gut* thing you won't need me when school starts and all my *schwestern* are back in the classroom."

"Speaking of," he said, tucking his thumbs into his suspenders. "I wondered if you'd be willing to be with Jacob in the fall while I plow and plant for the winter wheat?" When he noticed her face paled, he rushed on to say, "I'm not asking you to quit your job, and I understand coming after school and on the weekends would be too much, but I think it's time I got back into the field."

"Noah," she said, adjusting the box in her arms. "I am honored, but I don't think I'll be here come fall."

His brow wrinkled. He opened and closed his mouth until he found the right words. "What do you mean you won't be here in the fall?"

Her tongue darted out and moistened her lips. She glanced over her shoulder and then looked at the canning jars in the box containing different flavors of jelly for his son. "I haven't told my parents yet, but I think I'm going to go stay with a cousin in Emporia and go to an *Englischer* school."

His heart dropped to his feet. "What?"

"I gave it some thought, and I think it's the right course for me."

He shook his head. Jacob continued to hold the screen door open. His little feet shuffled beneath him, and Noah didn't mind if a fly flew in. "Jacob needs you."

"No," she said. "Jacob needs a *mamm*."

"I need you," he said, his voice barely registered to his own ear.

She touched his forearm, her fingers to his skin. Her warmth, her strength, her courage, her caring and her love. And she was going to take it all away. "You need a *fraa*, Noah."

Chapter Thirteen

Lydia's words felled him. Cut him to the core. And he didn't know what to say. He knew what he wanted to say, what he wanted to yell from the top of his lungs. But he couldn't.

A chorus of peeps reminded him he had work to do, and he pushed his emotions to the back of his mind. He picked up the crate and carried the chicks to the back porch and into what Collette had called the laundry room, where he'd placed the brooder. He hoped he wouldn't cross paths with Lydia. He wasn't sure he could see her and not beg her to stay in Garnett and marry him. He couldn't offer her marriage. Not as long as he was bound by the promise he'd made to Collette.

He dumped a bag of pine shavings into the brooder and pushed it around for an even layer. Food and water were placed on one side of the container, and a small makeshift perch. He'd purchased the supplies to prepare for getting chicks from Elam, but he was thankful Levi and Malachi had given him some from their stock. He turned on the heat lamp attached to a small battery. He crouched between the crate and the brooder and picked up one chick. "Hello, little one. Thank you for coming to our home."

He stroked the top of its head a few times and placed

it on the straw. It was too early to tell if the chicks were male or female, but he greeted each one the same, all while trying to keep Lydia's leaving from his mind.

When he was finished, he stood up and pulled a towel from the cabinet to place on the floor beside the brooder for Jacob to kneel on when he visited. It was then he noticed a black book tucked in the back of the cabinet. Curious, he pulled it out. He didn't need to open it to know what it was. Collette's Bible. What was it doing here? She must have placed it here while doing laundry and forgotten it. He recalled seeing her back here, sitting in a rocker near the windows. He'd long since placed the rocker in the empty room upstairs as it reminded him of her, holding Jacob in the crook of her arm while she read a book. She'd liked this room because it allowed a lot of natural light.

Noah tucked the Bible beneath his arm and exited the way he came. He found his way to the picnic bench and laid the Bible down as he sat. He stared at the black cover for several long seconds. Hope stirred around in his mind, and he wasn't sure what that looked like. For so long, bare-minimum halfhearted prayers had fueled his days. Believing *Gotte* had forsaken him and Jacob, he'd quit believing *Gotte* wanted to hear from him. He'd tried to remain thankful for his blessings, but he'd been afraid to seek *Gotte*'s wisdom. Too afraid of meeting silence. And too afraid his prayers and thanksgiving would fall on unhearing ears. He'd quit opening his Bible when he realized Collette wouldn't survive her cancer.

The black leather cover called to him, and he drew his fingers over the gold lettering. "What do you have to say to me, *Gotte*?"

A little white piece of paper peeked from the pages

and Noah turned to the marker. His name was scrawled on the little strip, with Isaiah 43:18-19. He scanned the scripture references until he found the spot.

He read the words aloud. "'Remember ye not the former things, neither consider the things of old. Behold, I will do a new thing; now it shall spring forth; shall ye not know it? I will even make a way in the wilderness, and rivers in the desert.'"

He sighed and ran his hand over his beard. "What new thing are you doing, *Gotte*? Can you even make a way for a man such as myself? One who was too self-centered for his own *gut*? Can you forgive me and make a way for me?"

He scrubbed his hands over his face and through his hair, dislodging his hat. Closing his eyes, he bowed his head as turmoil ricocheted through his heart. "I love Lydia. More than I ever thought I could. I've no doubt she is a gift, but is she a gift for me and my *sohn* or a gift to be known elsewhere?"

Lifting his head, he focused on the small strip of paper. His name. The scripture. A message for him, but what had Collette been trying to convey? Hope? If that was true, it still didn't absolve him from the promise he'd made. He couldn't tell anyone about Collette's secret. His secret. And that kept him bound to loneliness and isolation as he didn't think he could navigate the community and Jacob without Lydia's love and support.

"*Gotte*, forgive me for thinking this lot I've been dealt is unfair."

And the crux of it was, he didn't think Lydia wanted to leave. He saw the anguish, the unshed tears. At first, he wasn't sure why, but now he wondered if she held some affection for him and Jacob.

The only way he'd find out is if he asked her. And he wasn't sure he was brave enough to do that, but then again, what did it matter? Even if she had feelings for him, he couldn't act on them, and for good reason.

He grabbed the Bible and flipped through the pages, wondering if there were any more strips of paper with his name on them when they opened to 1 Corinthians 13. An envelope with *Lydia* scrawled in Collette's handwriting stared at him. The date, a week before her death, was printed at the bottom. What could possibly be written inside? His eyes caught the scripture he knew all too well. It was the scripture that drove him to marry a friend in trouble. A woman he didn't love in the way a man and woman should love each other. *Charity suffereth long, and is kind; charity envieth not; charity vaunteth not itself, is not puffed up, Doth not behave itself unseemly, seeketh not her own, is not easily provoked, thinketh no evil; Rejoiceth not in iniquity, but rejoiceth in the truth; Beareth all things, believeth all things, hopeth all things, endureth all things.*

Rejoiceth in the truth screamed at him, and he longed to tell Lydia the truth, but how could he? Even though it was his secret to keep, it wasn't his to tell.

He flipped through the Bible one more time to see if there were any other messages for him and, finding none, he closed it shut with a firm snap.

He stared at the envelope, turned it over in his hand, and debated whether or not to open it. He tapped it against his palm. It wasn't his to read. And even though he was curious, knowing it was probably the last thing his late wife had communicated with anyone, he made the decision to give it to Lydia before she left today. But first, he needed to at least tell her as much truth as he could without breaking his promise to Collette.

Lydia barely made it inside with the box and to the table before she collapsed onto one of the dining room chairs. She buried her face in her hands and let the tears fall. Jacob's small hand pulled on her sleeve. "K-d-d. K-d-d. Eat."

She lifted her head, dried her eyes and said, "Yes, we'll eat."

Pushing from the chair, she pulled out the jars and set them on the table. Jacob climbed onto the seat she'd just vacated. He cupped the jar of strawberry jelly and turned it. "Mmm, mmm."

Lydia opened the bread box and found a loaf of store-bought bread and made a mental note to make several loaves and stick them in the freezer. She found a knife, a spoon and a plate. "Would you like to help make your sandwich?"

His smile lit up the room and dispersed her sadness as much as it could be. She laid the bread on the plate, then opened all three jars. Jacob climbed down from the chair, opened the refrigerator and pulled out the grape jelly. Lydia couldn't help but giggle.

She grabbed a small tea plate and dropped a small spoonful of each jelly. She gave the spoon to Jacob. "Do you want to taste them?"

He laid the spoon down and dipped his index finger into the strawberry. Lydia noted his facial expression as the jelly hit his taste buds. He repeated the gesture with each one, before looking up at her.

"Here," she said, handing him the spoon. "Which one do you want on your bread?"

She was surprised when he scooped the spoon into the apricot and dropped the jelly onto the plate to the side of his bread. They spent the next twenty minutes working on making his sandwich, and it didn't bother her. Jacob ended up having apricot, grape and peanut butter on his bread. He grabbed the butter knife, and her instinct was to take it back, but she stopped herself and carefully watched him as he cut his sandwich like Noah did. Albeit somewhat off-center, but they were cut in two triangles.

"*Gut* job, Jacob," she said, clapping. "*Gut* job!"

She made her sandwich, and the two of them sat in silence as they ate. Jacob ate with a satisfied smile. Lydia was proud of what he'd accomplished, but ached from the pain churning in her heart.

"Should we make your *daed* a sandwich?"

Jacob fished his little hand into the opened end of the bread bag and pulled out one piece of bread, and then another. He laid them out and inched them up until they were meticulously in line with each other.

"*Gut,*" she said. "Now, which jelly should we give him?"

Jacob pulled each one close and then pushed them back, until he decided on strawberry. Lydia held the spoon out to him. "Do you want to put the jelly on?"

Jacob took the spoon, and after Lydia took off the lid, he dipped the spoon in and did his best to scoop some out. He plopped the jelly onto the bread, and Lydia added the peanut butter to the other slice. Jacob made a show of trying to cut the sandwich in half, so Lydia followed his miming instructions.

"There," she said. "All done, Jacob. You did a *gut* job. Your *daed* will be very happy. Shall we take it to him?"

"No need." Noah's voice sounded from behind them.

"Noah, you startled me," she said, glancing over her shoulder. His head was bare, and his brown hair stood at odd angles as if he'd been running his fingers through. He looked wild and untamed, and more handsome than ever, except he wasn't smiling. Had something happened? "You've lost your hat," she teased.

The lines of his mouth remained firm, flat, unsmiling. Her heart lurched.

"Me, me," Jacob repeated as he scrambled down from the table and clutched on to Noah's pant leg. When he pulled away to climb back onto his chair, she couldn't help noticing the jelly Jacob had left behind on Noah's pants.

"We made you a sandwich," Lydia said, motioning to his cut triangles. "But we would have brought it to you."

"I won't stay long," Noah said. His pain-filled eyes held her, and her heart cracked a little. "I need to tell you something, and I need you to listen to everything I have to say."

"Okay," she said, turning in her chair to fully face him.

"I love you."

Stunned, she froze. Everything in her stilled, except the roaring in her ears. Had she heard what she thought she heard? The words he'd spoken, words she'd longed to hear for so many years, belied his demeanor. She hoped she was reading his body language wrong, and energy vibrated through her. Her heart filled with joy. "I love you, too, Noah. And Jacob."

Shaking his head, he held his hand up to stop her from coming any closer. "I know. It shows in everything you do. Everything you've done for us. I love you, and I have for a long time." He paused. The man she'd seen when she'd first shown up last week, lost and alone, stood before her. Gone was the man whose brown eyes lit with exuberant joy while teasing her and playing with his *sohn.* Whatever he was about to say couldn't be good. Her heart began to break—not just break, but shatter into a million little pieces. Her hands shook, and she thought she might be ill.

"I would marry you if I could, but I can't. Not now. I would if I could." He looked longingly at her, and then at his *sohn.*

No longer able to hold them back, Lydia's tears streamed down her cheeks. When she'd reentered his life, she'd worried he was on the precipice of being lost to their community, and she'd wanted to give that back to him and Jacob. Her family and Levi had rallied around him to help restore what he'd lost when his birds became sick. Even Gideon had helped. This last week, Noah had been happy, a changed man. Reintegrating Noah and Jacob into their community had been working, giving them something back they needed. True, they'd only interacted with his family, hers, and Gideon, but their support was evident, and she'd hoped they could go to the market on Friday night when their community gathered around the square to sell their goods, and to Sunday service. Jacob needed the experience of being around people and crowds. She needed to see his reaction so she could format a well-thought-out plan for Jacob and Noah to better navigate overwhelming situations.

For a time, Noah had been his old happy, competitive and teasing self. Had she lost him?

"You said I needed a wife. We," he said, motioning between him and Jacob. His brown eyes, dark and stormy, were almost the color of brewed coffee just before cream was added. "We need you, but I can't act on that need, or our wants. Not yet, maybe never. I just thought you should know."

"I don't understand, Noah," she cried. "If we love each other, we can make it work. Whatever it is you say is keeping us from marrying, we can overcome it together. I can help you bear this burden you carry."

"Not in this. I don't see a way, Lydia. In fact, there is no way," he said.

"'I will do a new thing,'" she said, quoting the scripture she'd read this morning as she prepared for the day.

He paled, his eyes grew wide and his mouth worked to say something. His wide chest shuddered as he drew in a breath and she wanted to gather him in her arms and hug him, to smooth the anguish from his eyes, and kiss away the sadness turning his mouth downward.

"'Now it shall spring forth, shall ye not know it?'" she continued. "'I will even make a way in the wilderness, and rivers in the desert.' Noah, can you not believe *Gotte* will do a new thing, that He'll make a way for us?"

Shaking his head, he took a step in. "I've looked and searched in my heart for a way, Lydia, and there is none. I'm sorry. I'm sorry for you. I'm sorry for me, but most of all, I'm sorry for the little boy who deserves a *mamm* as wonderful and as patient and as loving as you are."

"Noah," she whispered, moving closer before he stopped her.

A white envelope shook in his trembling hand. He held it out to her. "I found this just now while preparing the brooder for the baby chicks. I don't know what it says or what it's about. It's yours. You can read it here, or take it home, but it's yours."

Her heart skittered to a halt when she saw her name written in Collette's handwriting. Almost four years after her friend's death. "Did she leave you one, too?"

Noah shook his head. "Jacob, would you like to see the chicks' new home?"

The little boy, unaware of the tension hanging in the room, was off the chair and out the door before Lydia blinked.

"We hope to see you tomorrow," Noah said, and then followed his son. "And if not, I understand."

She focused on the screen door as he disappeared down the stairs, feeling as if this would be the last time she saw him. Her heart ripped in two. The very thing she'd hoped for and dreamed about since she was a young girl of fourteen, when he'd bravely walked her home to face her *daed* after she'd fallen from the tree and broken her arm, had been realized and once again ripped from her all in a matter of a few minutes.

Collapsing onto the kitchen chair, she stared at the envelope through her tear-blurred eyes. The date indicated the letter had been written a week before Collette's death, a day after her friend had made her promise she'd take care of Jacob and Noah. A promise Lydia had failed to keep, and even though she was here now, it appeared she would have to break that promise. Knowing Noah loved her and wanted to marry her but couldn't because of a reason he refused to share with her, it would be too difficult to continue coming to his *haus* and maintaining propriety, even with her *bruders* and *schwestern* acting as chaperones.

Unable to wait any longer, she tore open the envelope. She blinked the tears from her eyelashes and wiped her eyes dry. More strolled down her cheeks as if they were in a buggy race and a coveted prize waited for them at the finish line. She sniffed and wiped her eyes again.

Dearest Lydia,
If you are reading this, I have left this Earth. Please don't grieve me as I know I'm in a better place and no longer suffering the illness that has wreaked havoc on my temporal being. Thank you for being the truest friend possible, even when it seemed like I betrayed you. I once told you one day you would understand, and today is that day. Yesterday, I made you promise you would look after Noah and Jacob for me, and I meant it. However, words failed me, and I could not expound. Knowing the cancer would take me soon, I grieved for my child and could no longer speak through the sadness.

Noah was never mine to hold. When he asked me to marry him, it wasn't out of love, but out of preservation of my reputation. You see, I had done the unthinkable and had found myself with child. He found me, suitcase in hand, walking along the side of the road after my parents had kicked me out. He is an honorable man. Jacob's father, not so much.

"What?" Lydia reread the lines, making sure she'd read them correctly and understood. Jacob wasn't Noah's child? She leaned back against the wooden spindles, feeling the curves press into her flesh through her dress.

I never would have told him, but he pulled it out from me, and to keep my parents from fully shunning me and being removed from the community, he offered to marry me, with the caveat that he would tell no one the truth about Jacob. It tormented me not being able to tell you, but it was the agreement we came to with my parents. I did it for Jacob's sake, to give him a home and a community without being labeled as a product of sin.

"Oh, Collette, how could you have not told me? I can't believe you went through this alone." No, not alone. She'd had Noah. Her beautiful, wonderful, stubborn-to-a-fault Noah.

Noah is honorable and everything that is gut. *I love him, but not in the way you think. He sacrificed for me, for my son. And if I know Noah, he will keep the secret until his own dying day. And if I know Noah as well as I think I do, he would never bring dishonor into a marriage by keeping secrets in his marriage. He loves you, Lydia. He told me before I agreed to marry him. He'd been prepared to court you with an eye to marriage, but he could not allow a friend to be run out of the community and suffer disgrace for an indiscretion such as mine.*

So, here I am, bearing my sins to you, hoping you will forgive me, but more importantly, love my child as your own, as I know you will. And convince Noah to marry you, because you are the most perfect fraa *for him.*

She laid the letter on the table. Blood roared in her ears, but not because she was angry. She hurt for her friend, and if Lydia had been in her shoes, she would have done anything to preserve her child's well-being, too. Even if it meant hurting others she loved. She dried her tears and moistened her lips. "Your secret is now mine to bear, Collette."

She glanced back at the letter.

One last thing. I know you were angry, but you had forgiven me in time. I also know you, maybe better than you know yourself, maybe better than Del knows you. I heard you cry out to Gotte *the other day while you thought I was sleeping. Asking for forgiveness. Somehow, my silly friend, you believe you wished this disease upon my body. You did not. My cancer is nothing more than the will of* Gotte. *You know that, and Noah knows that. You are not responsible for this. Let it go and go love that stubborn man of yours.*
Love, Collette

More tears blurred her eyes as she thought about Jacob. "*Denki*, for giving Noah and me the gift of Jacob."

Now all she had to do was convince that stubborn man of hers that he was a perfect helpmate for her.

Chapter Fourteen

Noah opened the Bible to where the piece of paper marked the passage Collette had left for him. Three days later he still reeled from Lydia quoting the scripture. There was no way she could have known the significance of the reference in Isaiah.

That could not have been a coincidence. Only *Gotte*. He just wished he could see beyond his current circumstances to what *Gotte* was about to do.

Hope had momentarily swirled in his chest, but unless he could tell Lydia the truth, he could never marry her. And there was no getting around that.

The last two mornings, Lydia had sent her *daed* and *mamm* to pick up Jacob. So she could avoid him. They didn't say as much, but Noah knew that was what she was doing. Just because she didn't want to see him didn't mean she would avoid Jacob.

The first day, Elam and Malinda had brought him the mature chickens, and when Jacob had asked for Lydia, they'd offered to take him to see her after they went to Butterfly Gardens.

Noah would be lying if he said he hadn't wanted to go, even if just to get a glimpse of Lydia or to hear her voice, but he hadn't been invited.

"What do you think, Jacob?" he said as he sat on the laundry room floor beside his *sohn*. "Do they like their new home?"

His *sohn*, the *kind* of his heart, smiled up at him. Noah might wish for things to be different now, but he didn't regret his decision to marry Collette and raise this child as his own. And even though his heart ached at not being able to marry Lydia, his mind would rest at night knowing he'd done the right thing by Jacob and Collette.

"Would you like to see the new chickens?" Noah asked as he climbed to his feet.

"D-d," Jacob said.

Shrugging, Noah said, "I don't know, *sohn*. I hope she comes today." But having not seen her for a few days, he wasn't sure. "Let's feed the chickens."

Jacob took his hand, and they walked out the back screened porch and headed to the newly built chicken coops. His heart swelled in gratitude at the help he'd received from the Beachy family, not just for the restoration of his business, but for restoring him back into their social network. He'd visited with Bishop Mueller yesterday and come up with a plan of action that suited him. He and Jacob would attempt church on Sunday, and if his child showed any signs of becoming overwhelmed, they'd leave as quietly as possible.

He opened the plastic trash bin and scooped some feed out. The hens squawked and pecked at the chicken wire housing them. He unlatched the lock and pushed his and Jacob's way into the coop. He handed Jacob the scoop and guided his hand as they shook the feed onto the ground. "*Gut* job, Jacob."

"Yes," Lydia said from behind him. "Very *gut* job."

Noah swiveled on his heels and drank her in like a man who'd gone without water for days in the middle of the hot summer. She was beautiful in her lavender dress, her white-blond hair tucked beneath her *kapp* with not a hair out of place. Her green eyes glittered, and he was happy to see they weren't red rimmed as they'd been the last time he saw her.

"D-d, D-d." Jacob grabbed for the latch.

Noah pushed open the door and let his son out. Jacob wrapped his arms around her legs, nearly knocking her over. "Be careful, Jacob. Don't hurt Lydia."

Releasing her, Jacob tucked his hand in hers. She smiled at Jacob. It was the smile of a mother looking at her child. His heart ached a little. Even though he knew he'd made the right decision, he mourned the fact Jacob would never know the love of a *mudder*. Especially one as loving and caring as Lydia.

"Hi," Noah said, dipping through the door of the chicken coop.

"Hi," she said.

"I didn't hear the buggy," he said. "I didn't know if you'd come." When she didn't respond, he glanced around the yard, looking for one of her *schwestern*. "Where are your sisters?"

"They didn't come today. *Mamm* and *Daed* are in the buggy. They wanted to take Jacob to the Hochstetlers with them, and then we can meet them at my house. Would you like to see sheep, Jacob?"

Jacob tugged on her hand, taking her toward the front of the house.

"I don't understand," Noah said.

"You will, but let's deliver this excited little boy to my parents first."

They strolled around to the front of the house, and once Elam was in sight beside the buggy, Lydia released his hand. Jacob's little feet and arms pumped as he raced toward the buggy. Lydia's *daed* assisted Jacob onto the seat next to Malinda and then tipped his hat at them as he waved.

"What's going on?" Noah asked.

"Can we sit out of the sun?" she asked, and before he could respond, she twined her fingers with his, their palms touching. In that moment, peace washed over him like he'd never known. It was temporary, and he should have pulled away, but it felt right. It felt good, and he just couldn't bring himself to pull away.

Lydia led him up the stairs and motioned for him to sit in one of the lawn chairs. She leaned against the porch railing and crossed her arms. "I think it's my turn to talk, and you listen."

"There's nothing you can say that will change my circumstances, Lydia," he said, feeling the weight of that truth crushing him. "No matter how much I wish it could be different."

"Where is your faith, Noah?" She uncrossed her arms and shifted the strap of her purse, until she had the black leather bag off her hip and against her stomach. "As I said, it's my turn to talk."

She fished out the envelope he'd handed her a few days ago from her purse. "First, I want to tell you what an amazing and *wunderbar* man you are. What you have done, the burdens you bore on your own... No one would have done what you have done. Not for someone they loved, and not for a friend. I only wish I had been as good a friend to Collette as you were."

He started to rise from his seat until she shook her head.

"I have a question for you and need you to be seated when I ask."

His forehead rippled. "Okay."

"Will you marry me, Noah Beiler?"

He slumped back against the chair. Raw emotions clawed at him. He was weary and tired of denying his love for this woman. He was tired of hiding from the community because his *sohn*'s abilities were limited. He sighed, thankful that Lydia had shown them things could be different. "I can't."

She knelt in front of him, laid the envelope on the porch and gathered his hands in hers. "If there were no barriers, nothing hidden between us, would you marry me?"

He rubbed his lips together and swallowed past the lump in his throat. "Without a doubt."

"Well, then," she said. "I was angry when you married Collette. You were supposed to ask to court me, and then you were married. To my best friend. My dreams shattered that day. Bitterness took root, and if I'm to be honest, I hated you and her for a time, but she asked for my forgiveness, and I gave it."

"I'm sorry," he said as he freed one of his hands and wiped a lone tear from her cheek.

"But I pushed aside my feelings for her. I helped her make her house a home and helped her prepare for Jacob. I stepped in and cared for her when the cancer became too much, often wondering why her family wasn't here, too."

He searched her eyes for any remaining animosity, but all he saw was sadness.

"When she died, I blamed myself." She bowed her head. "I believed the cancer was a result of my own prayers, not that I ever once wished Collette harm or ill will, but I couldn't help wondering if I inadvertently had, because my thoughts and heart had been so full of you.

"She asked me—no, she made me promise to care for you and Jacob when it was clear she was dying," she said, picking up the letter. "The day prior to writing this. If I'd somehow seen this four years ago, maybe things would have been different for us, but I've had some time to reflect and think, and consider, and I've come to a conclusion. If I'd seen this letter then, I wouldn't have been equipped with the experience I have now working with children like Jacob. I never would have walked into the school and applied for a job, and I wouldn't know how to cope. I realize *Gotte*'s ways are so much higher and more efficient than our own. He orchestrated all of this. You, me, Collette and Jacob."

He shifted in the mesh lawn chair and squeezed her hand. "That doesn't change things. I wish it did."

She handed him the letter. "This does. She told me everything, and I couldn't love you more. Your sacrifice for a friend, your selflessness, proves to me the kind of man you are, Noah. And I wouldn't want to marry any other man, as you are the most perfect *mann* a woman could ask for. You're the most perfect *mann* I could ask for." She released his hand and stood. "If after you read this, and you still feel there are barriers that would keep us from marrying, I will walk away and not press the issue, but if you decide I'm the *fraa* for you and the *mamm* for Jacob,

I'll be at the chicken coops. And for the record, Gideon and I never courted. I never had interest."

"The buggy ride after the singing—"

"Was not a buggy ride. No matter what you heard." She sighed. "I can't believe you even thought I would. Not intentionally. I was too wrapped up in Noah Beiler to know any other man existed. My buggy wheel broke. He took me home. Nothing more."

She descended the steps and disappeared, leaving him alone with Collette's last words. He opened the letter, noting the tearstains, and he wondered if they were Collette's, Lydia's or a mixture of both.

Lydia opened the latch on the chicken coop. "Hello, old friends. How are you liking your new home?"

She crouched and held her hand out, allowing the hens to brush their heads against her palm. After telling her *daed* she was going to ask Noah to marry her, she'd helped him handpick the best of the birds to help reestablish Noah's flocks.

When Noah gave his answer, she didn't want to waste any time preparing for a wedding. They'd gather at her family home in an hour, with his family, all his *bruders*, *schwestern*, and even Aunt Esther and celebrate their new beginning, not formally, as they would need to meet with Bishop Mueller and request their announcement be published, or rather announced to the community at church this coming Sunday.

She only prayed Noah would agree to another quick wedding. After waiting so long to be Noah Beiler's *fraa*, she didn't want to wait another day. It'd be torment waiting until fall, but given the circumstances with Jacob, she hoped the bishop would allow them to marry quickly like Abe and Naomi had.

She sensed Noah's approach before she heard him. Unfolding to her full height, she turned and watched him stroll toward her.

"Do you approve of the birds?" he asked.

"I do." She motioned toward the letter as she stepped out of the coop. "We should burn it."

He hesitated, his hand shaking, but nodded. "I agree."

She took his hand and was relieved when his palm relaxed against hers. "The secret is safe with me."

"*Denki*," he said. "For everything, and I'm sorry—"

"For being honorable? Don't," she said.

They stopped at the burn barrel, and Noah opened a toolbox next to it and pulled out a book of matches.

"Are you sure?" he asked, handing her the envelope. "It's your letter."

"I'm sure." She pulled out the letter and crumpled it into a ball before handing it back to Noah.

He leaned over the barrel and held the balled paper inside as he struck a match and let the corner catch fire. Lydia allowed the envelope to fall from her hand and join the letter. They watched in silence until every bit of paper turned to ash.

Noah turned to her and took her in his arms. He kissed her brow. "Yes, Lydia Beachy, I will marry you."

She leaned back and looked into his beautiful brown eyes. She loved this man, who'd taken on a child and loved him like his own, and she probably always had. "*Gut*, because our families are waiting for us at my house, and we have an appointment with Bishop Mueller this afternoon to request the announcement be published this

Sunday. I hope you don't mind. I've waited a long time for this moment."

His gaze dropped to her mouth, and she knew he wanted to kiss her. She touched her fingers to his lips and smiled. "Soon, my love. Soon."

Epilogue

Lydia stretched her back as she climbed to her feet and stood back to look at the work she'd completed. It was against their practice to carve names into gravestones, but the least she could do was keep Collette's resting place tidy. She'd rolled the cinder block away and cleaned up the weeds that had grown around it. When her husband joined her, they'd dig a hole and set the new stone.

"*Ammi, ammi*," she heard Jacob call her, and her heart warmed. She and Noah had been married almost four months now, and Jacob calling her by his endearment and recognizing her as his *mamm* never failed to bring great pleasure to her heart.

Jacob fell to his knees and began playing in the dirt. Noah wrapped his arms around her midsection, and she leaned back against him. "How is planting going?"

"Better, now that I'm here with you. I stopped by the *haus* to grab Jacob from Jessie so she could finish baking her cookies without our *sohn* under foot." he said as he kissed her. "And how are you?"

"*Gut.* I'm glad to have this done," she said. "All that's left is for you to place the headstone, but that can wait until tomorrow. Our families will be here soon, including your cousins Levi, Abe, Malachi and their families."

"Let's hope the weather remains reasonably warm," he said. "If not, I can always start a fire. By the way, the quilt you made for Jacob is wonderful."

"That sounds nice."

"We can always cancel," he whispered.

"No." She shook her head. "Jacob has looked forward to seeing his cousins and friends all day."

"And I have looked forward to holding my *fraa* all day."

"Patience, my love, patience," she said covering his hands with hers.

His laughter rumbled through her. "You think to use the tactics you use on Jacob on me?"

She turned and wrapped her arms around his neck and then kissed him. "No, but I need to help my *schwester* prepare the kitchen and get the tables set up outside."

"What's left to do?" he asked. "Jacob and I can help."

She gave him the list of what she wanted to accomplish. As they walked back to the house, she could smell the churned fields. The renewing of life. She touched her palm to her stomach as she smiled. "When will the winter wheat be ready to harvest?"

"Next June, maybe July, depending on the weather," he said, as he reached for her hand.

"*Gut*," she said.

"Why? Do you have plans?"

"Maybe," she said, and then releasing her hand from his she tapped his arm. "Tag, you're it. Run, Jacob!"

She hitched up her skirts a little and ran as Noah and Jacob chased after her. Noah caught her by the waist, turned her toward him and kissed her.

"What do you mean by maybe?" he asked, his brown

eyes dancing with mischief. "You promised to help bear my burdens. I expect you to be right by my side, my beautiful wife."

Jacob grabbed hold of them, and stepped on one of her feet, his other on Noah's. "Me, me."

"I will always be right by your side, my husband, unless I'm tending to our *boppli*."

"Our what?" he asked, his mouth gaping like a fish out of water.

"Baby, baby," Jacob said, releasing them as he jumped up and down.

"Yes, our baby," Lydia said as she pecked her husband's cheek. "I love you, Noah Beiler. I think I always have."

"I love you, too, Lydia, and I couldn't be happier," he breathed against her lips. "*Denki*, *Gotte*, for doing a new thing."

* * * * *

If you liked this story from Christina Rich, check out her previous Love Inspired books:

A Husband for an Amish Bride
A Family for the Twins
The Marshal's Unexpected Bride

Available now from Love Inspired!
Find more great reads at www.LoveInspired.com.

Dear Reader,

I hope you enjoyed *The Amish Widower's Dilemma* as much as I did writing it.

I cannot tell you how much the autistic world means to me, and this story really comes from the heart. All three characters stem from life experiences in many different ways. If you're interested in knowing more, follow my blog at www.authorchristinarich.com or sign up for my newsletter where I'll talk more about some of those experiences.

There is a quote by Paul Gallico: "It is only when you open your veins and bleed onto the page a little that you establish contact with your reader." I hope you sensed that connection because there was a lot of bleeding from the writer vein, there was also a lot of joy being able to show Noah's growth and enlightenment when he realizes he can enjoy his son and that not every day has to be hard.

I love to connect with readers, and would love to know what part of Noah and Lydia's story touched you most.

Blessings,
Christina Rich